MW01147253

Arrivals and Depart Christopher Jennings Penders is a beautiful, haunting collection of seven stories set on one of the most spectacular and pristine places in North America —and a favorite getaway for the author. As the title suggests, the collection is a tribute to the magic of Block Island, just off the Rhode Island shore.

Each of the stories is about arrivals and departures-- a cohesive metaphor for the lives of people in transition and in need of physical and spiritual healing. With a lovely touch of magical realism, nearly each of the stories is gently charged with a supernatural presence.

The magic of the island and each of Penders' tales is how old lives cross new, sometimes taking the form of reincarnated spirits, but not of the horror kind. Yes, there are weird apparitions, haunted light houses, disembodied voices in the dark, ominous threats in the night. But Penders' ghosts are not revenants from The Bad Place. His Block Island is The Good Place, where long dead promises are fulfilled; where crippling doubts and failings are redeemed; where lonely, private people find spiritual fulfillment and love.

In each of these graceful, well-crafted tales, Block Island proves to be different things to different characters- -a spiritual sanctuary, escape from turmoil and grief, a coming home, a renewal.

As the last line in the collection declares, "Magic permeated Block Island. You could find it anywhere. You only need to know where to look." But not in the magical landscape or eternal sea, but within.

Gary Braver, bestselling and award-winning author of *Tunnel Vision* and, with **Tess Gerritsen**, *Choose Me*.

Author & Publisher Note on the Cover Photo

While walking along the beach behind the Surf Hotel on Block Island, I came across a white stone on the sand. I was immediately drawn to it because it was the only stone within yards. It stood out. I started focusing my camera and took several pictures. The single stone represents Block Island, and the sand represents the Atlantic Ocean.

– C. Jennings Penders

When it came time to think about cover art for this collection of stories, I asked Chris Penders to present me with photographs from his photographic archive since Chris is not just a writer, he's also a photographer. I thought it would be a neat idea to showcase one of Chris' photographs, rather than the work of a third party. His first thought was a photograph of Southeast Light, but I felt that was an overdone image in the public eye. He then sent me the photo that appears on the cover. It spoke to me immediately. I thought of metaphor, one of the most important ingredients of literature: the lone stone is like an island amidst a sea of sand. As sometimes people are alone too, yet always connected by unseen forces.

– The Publisher

Arrivals and Departures:

An Etheric Tribute
to Block Island

C. Jennings Penders

Guilford, Connecticut

This is a work of fiction. Although many of the settings and locations are real, and some of the characters are based on real people (by permission) all other characters and incidents are derived from the author's imagination. Any resemblance to actual persons living or dead is purely coincidental. The publisher assumes no responsibility whatsoever for the thoughts, views, or ideas expressed by the author.

Published by Fahrenheit Books
An imprint of OmicronWorld Entertainment LLC
42 Water Street, Suite 222
Guilford, CT 06437
203.453.5700

www.OmicronWorld.com
OmicronWorldEnt@yahoo.com

Cover design by Christopher Dobbins, C.E.D. Design & Productions.
Cover photo by C. Jennings Penders. Used by permission.

**A FAHRENHEIT BOOKS TRADE PAPERBACK ORIGINAL
FIRST EDITION 30 October 2020**

Edited by Timothy Jacobs & Jennifer Christiansen of
JWC Publishing.

ISBN-13: 978-0-9968784-5-6 (Trade paper)
ISBN-13: 978-0-9968784-7-0 (Kindle/Mobi)
ISBN-13: 978-0-9968784-6-3 (EPub)

Contents

Introduction   9

Fire at the Ocean View   15

Arrivals and Departures   47

Mad Maggie   88

Night Swimming   116

Magnetic North   158

Together   202

End of Season   238

Acknowledgements   253

Introduction

In November 2018 during the Q&A session at my book launch for *Taking Off a Coat* and *Random Acts,* an important question was asked. Sherri Ashburner, an old friend I worked with at RJ Julia Booksellers in Madison, Conn., asked, "Have you ever considered writing fiction again?

I'd become so intent on writing for Wisdom and Life (my spiritual blog), that the thought of writing fiction seemed as far away as Mars in March 2019. A short four months later, I became immersed in this new collection of short stories that you hold in your hands. I put my blog on hiatus and started writing fiction again at full bore.

It certainly helps that I'm writing about my favorite place. Since it's been a location I've loved for a long time, I try to visit Block Island every summer. What's nice is that even when I'm not there, I still feel like I am when I'm writing. I can go there in my head.

I have several complete and incomplete novels sitting around. I now understand that I don't have the ability to maintain time continuity with the characters in each of my novels. As a way to correct that, I have created this new collection. Here's how I did that: When you read this collection, you'll find multiple characters returning throughout the book. You get to see them grow in their friendships with others.

A few of the recurring characters are based on real people. Bruce Pigott, a chef in real life, is someone I graduated high school with. He worked at the Saybrook Fish House. However, since I haven't seen him since high school, I've given him traits and personality he probably does not exhibit today.

My nephews, Sean and James, and my nieces, Rylee and Teagan, also appear in this collection as adult versions of themselves. They are all under the age of ten in 2020. My brother, John (Sean and James's dad), flies the C-130. In this collection, I've attempted to create authenticity around the characters who are based on real people. Of course, I can't be relied on to be factual about every point. This is a work of fiction after all.

❖ ❖ ❖

Everyone has a favorite place. Somewhere they feel as if they belong. Somewhere their soul sings out in a location where they get goose bumps every time they arrive. If you're lucky, your soul-place is close by, so you can return with great frequency to replenish, recover, and let your soul sing out.

Anyone who *really* knows me understands where my soul-place is. For those of you who aren't familiar enough with me, I'll let you in on my secret. It's Block Island, Rhode Island! When I was a young boy, my maternal grandparents brought me to Block Island for the first time. As soon as my feet touched the ground, I felt an electric current pass through me. It was like something inside me said: *Yes! You're home!*

Being all of ten or eleven years old at the time, I didn't understand the feeling. I only knew I felt serene; a calm came over me and I remember smiling the widest grin. I ran up Payne's Dock where the Block Island Ferry landed in the early 1970s, my outstretched arms trying to grab at the fresh clean air. My grandmother stood behind, watching me. I glanced back and saw her smile as well. It was my first time on Block Island, and I didn't know it at the time, but it would also be my last for almost twenty years.

That afternoon on the ferry ride back to New London, sitting between my grandparents, my grandmother looked at me and took my hand. She smiled again and said, "When I saw you run up the dock today, I knew we made the right decision coming here. You seemed so happy. When we walked through town, I'd glance over at you and that smile was always plastered across your face."

Those weren't her exact words but the general idea is there. I carried that day with me for as long as I could, but as with all memories, it faded into the cloth that became worn and tattered over the many years I've had it stored away. Then in the early 1990s, my friend Jason reintroduced me to Block Island. He and I took a day trip there, and once again, the moment my feet touched the island, everything flooded back from that day so long ago with my grandparents: my running up Payne's Dock, the stupid grin on my face all day. I looked over at Jason and the smile returned. I was home again.

As we spent the day driving all over the island, I never felt so alive. Since rediscovering Block Island with Jason during that first trip, it's become a pilgrimage to return every year. I've only missed two years, 2008 and 2020, the latter because of the COVID-19 pandemic. Funny, how attached we become to places. Looking back now at my first trip to Block Island with my grandparents, I can clearly see why my soul sings out when I'm there.

Besides writing, I'm an avid photographer and have an entire collection of Block Island photography at my website:

www.cjpphotos.com/blockisland

In April 2019, I began formulating a plan to write a book with Block Island as the setting. But as I said at the beginning, I realized I couldn't carry one thought, one storyline through an entire novel. Instead, I used recurring characters to tie the book together in seven short stories. I hadn't attempted to write fiction since the early 1990s, and I felt a little intimidated returning to that field after having spent over ten years blogging about spirituality and the Law of Attraction.

However, once I started writing, I realized as long as I loved what I wrote about, my fiction muse would return. And return it did. I'm once again fully engaged in fiction writing. Another Block Island collection may be forthcoming, we shall see. In the meantime, I sincerely hope you enjoyed your time here.

C. Jennings Penders
Madison,CT
May 2020
www.cjenningspenders.com

Fire at the Ocean View

Jennifer was determined to make the best of her week on Block Island. As the ferry docked at Old Harbor Landing, she breathed in the cool, salt air, which dispelled the last trace of her reluctance. She had picked the perfect day to start a vacation. The sun was out and people congregated at the pier, greeting friends and family. Surf pounded the nearby beach and a breeze blew in from the water, splaying her blond hair around her misty blue eyes. As she admired the view, she tucked the fly-aways under her New York Yankee's baseball hat.

Jen stood on the ferry's top deck. From there, she could see pleasure boats come and go. She looked down through the clear salt water. Fish swam by. Fiddler crabs danced across the ocean's floor. She even glimpsed a lobster on the seabed. As she watched in dazed amusement, something tugged at the back of her mind. She glanced out at the island and was struck by how familiar it felt.

Jen was happy she had finally taken Lisa's advice. Lisa had visited the island and told Jen what a special place it was. She brought pictures back, trying to convince her to go, but there was always an excuse why she could not go. Jen was a celebrity, and she couldn't go anywhere without someone gawking. That's why she left the center stage and took a more subdued job at Swan Song, a New York based magazine that published cutting edge fiction. "What if I'm recognized? The island is so small." Or, "See all this work here? How do you expect me to leave this?"

"You'll be so relaxed once you get there, you'll forget about everything," was Lisa's reply.

Jen loved her job at the magazine. She spent two days a week reading from the slush pile even though she had been promoted and finding new talent wasn't technically part of her daily tasks anymore. But she loved how it felt when she was lost in somebody else's world. On Mondays and Fridays, she went to the mailroom and grabbed a box of stories. She'd return to her sparkling new office, espresso maker whirring, and sift through manuscripts.

She had numerous friends, but if one thing was lacking, it was someone to share her life with. Sure, Lisa was there, but friendship was different. It was another often-used excuse for delaying her vacation plans. "I don't want to go away on my own." Lisa managed to use this in her favor. It was what finally convinced Jen to go.

One night, while Jen was working late, the office phone rang unexpectedly around 9 PM. She also did not answer, but found her hand reaching for the receiver.

"Hello, this is Jen, editor at Swan Song."

The voice on the other end was exasperated. "You know Jen, you spend too much time working," Lisa's voice said in the receiver. "If you keep this up, you're going to end up alone, like an old spinster. I'm sure you don't want that. You need this vacation."

Of course, Lisa was right.

❖ ❖ ❖

Before leaving New London, Lisa gave her an itinerary that included a big pink highlighter splash across the word *Finn's*.

"Get their lobster roll," she'd said as she reached out for a hug. "You won't be disappointed." She took a step back and looked at the ferry as passengers began to board. "God, I wish I was going. Don't forget, check-in at the Spring House is at eleven o'clock. I've booked you for a week and you're on the 1 PM ferry home next Sunday. Have a wonderful time."

Jen looked a little flustered, then said, "Oh, by the way, thanks again for letting me crash at your place. So much better than trying to drive up from New York at God knows what hour."

Lisa smiled. "You're welcome anytime."

Seeing Jen's uncertain facial expression, Lisa added, "And don't worry about the magazine. We'll survive."

The hour-long ferry ride was surprisingly refreshing. Jen had not been on a boat in years, and the crisp salt air felt like a tonic.

As the ferry entered the breakwater harbor Jen felt relaxed, but she also experienced a sudden sense of déjà vu. It felt as if she been here before. No. Foolish. I've never been here before, Jen thought.

As she drove her Subaru off the ferry, she made up her mind that she would indeed forget about the magazine for a week and enjoy her vacation.

She found a parking stall in the nearby public lot and walked to Finn's Seafood.

Jen hoped her baseball cap and shades provided enough of a disguise. It did not. As she walked through the crowd, she bumped into a young man and her hat fell to the ground. The guy stooped down to retrieve it. When he handed her the hat, his eyes opened wide. "You're…"

Damn you, Lisa.

She nodded to the young man as a small crowd started gathering.

"See now," she said under her breath, "this is why I left modeling."

She managed to push her way through the crowd and most disperse, but several people remained close, following her.

Another young man stopped her and asked, "Can I get a picture with you?"

Jen drew in a breath. "Alright," she said. "Just one."

The guy smiled and grabbed someone in the crowd. He handed the stranger his camera and asked, "Will you take our picture?"

This caused more people to stop, and Jen sighed on the inside while smiling so as not to appear rude. Even here on Block Island, she could not escape her fans.

She decided to forget the picture-taking guy and make the most of her trip. The tangy salt air invigorated her as she breathed it in.

What a difference between this and New York, she thought.

In Manhattan it felt at times like you were smoking a pack of cigarettes with each breath. And the odors! In summer the streets smelled like a combination of sour milk and cat litter.

Thinking of the city — even its pollution and constant crowds — made her think of her favorite late-night burrito joint, and waking up early for work. The city — despite its problems — was her comfort zone. Now she had doubts again about being on this island.

When she approached Finn's takeout window, she boosted her spirit and put on a smile. Seeing the sun shining off the water and the occasional cloud drifting overhead, she decided she would eat outside.

A young man approached from behind the counter with a drink in his hand. "Hi, welcome to Finn's," he said, putting the glass on the counter. "What can I get you?" It took him a moment, but then he smiled. "Jen Cartwright, right?"

She rolled her eyes. "It's been five years since my last job. How the hell does everyone still recognize me?"

"It isn't so hard, Miss Cartwright. You were on the cover of Vogue, at least, what, like three times. What made you quit modeling?"

"This," she said. "I couldn't escape. I finally have a career I really enjoy and I'm respected for more than my looks. That's why I quit modeling."

"Well, I hope you don't mind my saying so, but I for one miss seeing your smiling face peering out at me."

Blushing now, Jen smiled, showing why she made such a lasting impression on the public. Her teeth were preternaturally white and straight. She still had the complexion of someone a decade younger than her thirty-six years. Her blond hair highlights and blue eyes were what everyone dreamed about. A part of her did miss this attention, but a very small part. "Thank you," she said. Jen adjusted her hat. Even after the sea winds on the boat ride had strewn her hair around, she still looked perfectly kempt, like she had just stepped out of a magazine shoot. "How about a lobster roll?" she asked, with a forward smile. "I hear they're the best on the island. And a Coke."

That smile still worked on everyone. The man behind the window smiled back, wrote her order down and handed her a stone with the numeral five painted on it. "Your order will be up in a few minutes. Don't forget to return the stone."

She nodded and walked to the eating area, noticing the seagulls chirping overhead. As she watched an older man throw a piece of bread into the air, and the gull grab it in flight, Jen found a chair and sat down.

Instantly, she realized the table was already occupied and began to apologize. She stood up to move to another table but instead she found herself staring at a young man for several seconds, frozen to the spot and unable to look away. He glanced up from his laptop and smiled. "Hi," he said, removing his dark sunglasses. His dark brown hair was cut short and his skin very tanned. When he removed his sunglasses, Jen couldn't help but stare into his bright green eyes. When she saw he had a five o'clock shadow, her heart jumped. Woah, she thought. Where did that come from? And when he smiled? Well, that almost put Jennifer over the edge. His smile was captivating.

"I'm Eric Thomas, by the way." He held out a hand.

She still couldn't take her gaze away from him. There seemed to be a magnetic hold on her. Now she smiled. "God, I'm sorry. I was watching that man

feeding the seagulls. I thought this table was empty."
She shook his hand "I'm Jen."

"Number five!" the voice over the loudspeaker rang
out.

"That's my order. Sorry to have interrupted you,
Eric. I'll let you get back to work." She started to rise,
then turned back. "Did you say your name was Eric
Thomas?" She removed her own sunglasses and
glanced at his computer.

"Yeah."

"Okay, I know that name. Mind if I ask what are you
doing there?" She nodded at his laptop.

He closed the computer. "Actually," he said,
scratching the stubble on his chin, "I'm finished for
now, but I'm working on a novel. I usually write short
stories, but this idea is too big to stay in the confines of
a short piece."

"Short stories?" she said, raising her brow.

"Number five, your order is ready!" hollered the
voice a second time.

Jen got up and started to walk away when Eric said,
"Won't you come back and join me. If you'd like to, that
is."

It felt right and she didn't hesitate to say "I'll do
that."

She returned with her food and set her tray down.
"So, what are you writing now?" she asked, before
biting into her sandwich. Soon her face had butter on it,
as graceful as she was trying to be.

"Here, you have butter on your chin." Eric pointed to where the butter started dripping down. When she kept missing the spot on her own, he took a napkin off her tray and reached across the table. "Making a mess is one of the amenities of eating lobster. Do you mind?"

She held her chin out as the napkin slipped from his hand, causing him to touch her face. A small, electric pulse, fluttered between them. It was almost like a current. He immediately withdrew his hand and stared at Jen.

She stared back, rubbing her cheek. "Did you feel that?"

He nodded and was about to continue, when something cracked on the pavement just outside Finn's eating area.

Jen turned to see a dead crab lying on the road. "What the heck was that?" she said. The strange experience they had now momentarily forgotten.

Eric grinned. "It's just a seagull. See," he said, nodding to the bird flying overhead. "They pick up crabs on the beach and drop them from the sky."

"That scared me." She laughed. "I hope he wasn't aiming for me."

Eric smiled. "Aren't you gonna eat?"

As islanders passed the two, they looked back and smiled. Word spread quickly on a small island, especially when celebrities arrived on the shore. Two women stood outside the patio and whispered to each other while sneaking pictures on their cellphones.

Others just stared, mouth agape, before moving on. A few were brazened enough to walk up to Jen, pieces of paper in their hands. "Can I get an autograph, Ms. Cartwright?"

Jen's cheek still tingled where Eric's finger had touched her. She took her hat off and placed it on the table. "Obviously this won't help me." She glanced at Eric. "I used to model. I thought, wrongly of course, that I would have been forgotten by now."

"Used to?"

She nodded, choosing not to elaborate. "Remember earlier I said I recognized your name?" Jen took a good-sized bite from her lobster roll and washed it down with a large gulp of her Coke. "I published one of your stories last month. I'm the editor at Swan Song. When I left modeling, a friend of mine worked at the magazine. She knew I did some editing for my high school and college papers, so she called me."

He raised his brow and laughed out loud. "You're *that* Jen Cartwright?" he said, shaking his head. "I thought your name sounded familiar too." He grew quiet for a moment. Finally taking a breath, he asked, "So, what brings you to Block Island? It's a haul from Manhattan Island."

Jen sipped from her drink again. "My friend, Lisa comes here every summer and raves about the island. I decided to see what the excitement is about. I'm glad I did." She put her drink down and smiled.

Their conversation seemed to be going well. "I'm glad too. Are you staying long?"

"I'm here for a week. I have a room at the Spring House."

Eric smiled. "Oh, you'll love it there. My friend Tom Norris owns the place.

"I'm looking forward to it." Jen smiled and glanced at her phone noting the time. "Speaking of the Spring House, it's check-in time."

Eric looked a Jen as she stood and grabbed her bag. "How about I go with you to the Spring House, introduce you to Tom. And I hope this doesn't sound too forward, but after you check in, I'd like it if we went for a walk together. How does that sound?"

"It does not sound forward. I did buy one of your stories, so you are one of my authors now." She smiled.

"Great! If you want to hang tight for a minute or two, I'll go get my car."

"No need. I have my car."

She took her hat, put it on, and shrugged. Even though there was an undeniable attraction, Jen was still a bit reluctant to go off with someone she had just met, and she now second-guessed herself for accepting his invitation so graciously. She stood rooted to the spot for several long moments unsure of what to do. "Do you normally pick up strangers so quickly?" she asked, before laughing in an attempt to show she meant it as a joke.

"I don't bite, promise. Besides, there seems to be a connection here. You feel it too, don't you?"

Finally, after another moment of indecision, she agreed. "Yes, I do. Maybe it will jar loose this feeling I have."

"What feeling?"

The wind picked up and blew her hat off. "I don't know. Maybe it's my imagination," she said, as she retrieved her cap, "but I feel like I've been here before. What do you plan on doing with your computer?" She put her sunglasses back on.

"I'll leave it with my brother. He works here."

Eric took the computer in one hand, and as he turned to walk toward the order window, his free hand brushed against Jen's. They looked at each other quickly, for once again something passed between them that was just as powerful as the first touch, yet something now familiar. Their skin buzzed, like the hum of a fluorescent light.

Jen shook her head. "You know," she said, "I can't ever recall feeling so comfortable with someone I only just met." Her eyes twinkled above her broad smile.

Eric's mouth dropped open. "I was going to say the same thing."

When they approached the window, Eric yelled in, "Hey."

The same guy who waited on Jen returned. "Why didn't you tell me you knew Jen Cartwright?" he said and took a sip of water from a glass that sat on the counter.

"Jen, meet my brother, Bill."

Jen flashed a smile and said, "Nice to meet you."

Eric handed the laptop through the window. "Here big brother," he said, "can you hold this for me? And take care of it this time." He glanced at Jen and said, "Last time he put the damn thing in the staff's coat room. Anyone could have walked off with it."

"No one did, though." Bill smiled at Jen and returned his drink to the counter. "So, how long have you known my brother?"

Jen's sunglasses kept slipping to the bridge of her nose and she pushed them up again. "We just met."

Bill laughed. "Riggght. You sat at that table for a whole hour, chatting away." He looked away. "I was guessing you two knew each other for years."

"Okay. If we really knew each other for years, where have I been hiding her?" Eric asked, playfully scratching his chin.

Bill shrugged.

"Why hasn't her name ever come up?"

Again, Bill shrugged. "So, maybe it hasn't been that long, but you know island gossip. Spreads like wildfire."

Eric sighed. "Whatever. Let them talk, just don't listen. I'll tell you if I have something important to say. You can count on it."

Bill smiled at Jen again. "You could be good for him, you know. He spends more time in front of his damn computer than he does anything else." He smiled at Eric, then turned to Jen again. "I keep telling him he's gotta get out and explore more. He's never gonna meet anyone if all he does is sit and writes all day."

Eric looked over at Jen. "I'm gonna show Jen around." "And, you know how it goes. If you're not careful, you're going to wake up one day and realize you're all alone."

Eric took her hand to help her up, but she refused to move. She stared back; her eyes wide at Bill. "What did you just say?"

"Eric's gonna wind up alone if he's not careful, like an old bachelor."

"Okay," she said, turning to Eric. "Now this is just plain weird. Lisa said the same thing to me a few days ago. She said I'd end up alone when old."

"Who's Lisa?" Bill wanted to know.

Eric smiled. "Jen's the head editor at Swan Song. Lisa's her assistant."

"That's weird. You do know that Eric just had a piece published in your magazine?" His eyes opened wide. "Wait a minute, I knew you two knew each other! What is this, a first date?" Bill turned to the kitchen staff. "I'll be right back. I gotta take this outside" Then to Eric, he said, "Wait for me. I'm coming out." He walked through the kitchen and the bar before stepping outside. "Now wait a minute. Let me get this straight.

When did you start keeping secrets from me?" He faced Jen. "Tell me the truth."

"Honestly, it's completely coincidental," Jen giggled. "You can trust me. I have a reputation to uphold here."

Eric looked at Jen. When she didn't flinch, he backed down. "Fine. So, you're an editor?"

She nodded.

Now he turned to Eric. "And you're a writer?"

"As if you didn't know."

Bill looked around Finn's. "Where is it?" he said, smiling.

Eric adjusted his glasses. "Where is what, Bill?"

"The hidden camera."

Jen laughed and looked around.

Bill ran his fingers through his hair. "Odd," he said, shading his eyes from the sun. "I was wrong. It's not a hidden camera show, it's a screenplay by Rod Serling."

A line formed at the takeout window and someone called out to him. "I'll be right there," he said before turning to Eric. "I gotta go, but I wanna hear more about this later."

Eric nodded. "Sure." He turned to Jen. "That's my brother for you. He gets a bit excited sometimes and doesn't know when to take it down a level." Now he smiled at Bill. "Go on," he said with a laugh. "Get back to work before you're fired."

Bill rolled his eyes at the brotherly taunt. He stood there, unwavering, and stared.

As they walked away, Jen looked to Eric, adjusting her Yankee cap. "I know this is going to sound strange, but this doesn't just happen. I mean, how strange is it that I published your work and that I met you the moment I arrived."

"I don't think that sounds strange at all," Eric said. "I feel like we've known each other for years." Eric reached for Jen's hand, and she took it. They interlaced fingers.

Three girls and two boys in their early teens stood across the street near the public lot. A lanky girl in jean shorts and a tube top leaned against a streetlight. She pulled out a pack of cigarettes and a lighter and began to distribute them to the crowd."

Eric winced. "See that? These kids have nothing better to do than hang out and smoke? Where the hell are their parents?" Jen smiled forgivingly.

"Hey, at least here, kids are only smoking. If this were New York...well anything goes."

Jen steered them away from the sidewalk toward the car lot. Walking along the road, Eric noticed he felt more comfortable than he had in years. He didn't quite know why, but Jen Cartwright fit. It was odd that he felt this way because he certainly wasn't looking for a relationship right now. I mean, relationship? Why was he thinking that? They had only just met.

Jen led him over to her red Subaru Outback. "Here we are," she said, reaching in her pocket for her keys. She opened the driver's side door, then leaned over the seat and unlocked the passenger door. "Alright. So, you'll have to tell me how to get to The Spring House."

"Go out here and take a left up at the rotary statue."

Once there, he directed, "Now straight up the hill to the Spring House. Big red roof, can't miss it."

Jen drove slowly as people walked alongside the road even though there were sidewalks. Mopeds zipped by at incredible speeds and bikers pedaled all around. It was a mix of fast and slow. "This is crazy. How do islanders cope in this traffic? I thought driving in New York was a challenge."

Eric shrugged his shoulders. "I guess we're just used to it. See that place with the red roof there on your right? That's where you want to pull in."

When parked, she stepped out and pulled her two rolling suitcases from the back. "May I?" Eric extended his hand offering to take one suitcase from her.

"Thanks."

Eric stood by her side and the two of them walked up the stairs to the long font porch.

"Hey, Eric. Good to see you. How's that book coming?"

"Slow going." He turned to Jen. "Tom, this is Jen Cartwright. She has a reservation here for a week. Can you help her?"

At forty-two, Tom still dressed as if he were in his early twenties, shorts and a tee shirt, not like a business owner at all. His shoulder length salt and pepper hair was unkempt and didn't exactly project an air of profession. It had become a running joke between them. "You should really clean yourself up," Eric said, "especially if you want to attract a better clientele." Built like a tank, strong, stout and muscular, your first impression of him would be to run in the other direction. When you got to know him however, you'd understand he was far more the pussycat then the army tank. It only took a few moments to realize Tom was harmless. If crossed though, he'd reluctantly show his anger.

He gave right back. "I think I'm doing just fine. Why last month, I booked the governor of Massachusetts and he's returning in August. And that's after he met me. Why don't you come this way Jen? I'll get your room key card and you can get rid of those bags." By the way, how do you know Jennifer Cartwright?" Tom asked as he turned to Eric.

"That's a funny story I'll share with you later. Jen and I are going for a walk after she checks in."

Tom grinned. "Alright," he said. "I look forward to hearing that." He strolled over to the front desk, reached under, and handed Jen her key card. "Enjoy Block Island." He gestured to Eric. "You have an amazing tour guide there."

After Jen dropped off her bags in her room, she returned to the lobby and found Eric near the stone fireplace in the sitting area. "Where are we going? Do we need to drive?"

"It's not too far. We can definitely walk from here. There used to be a hotel but it burnt down, so it's just an empty lot now. I go there when I need to think. And, I think, it feels right to share it with you."

Jen stopped in mid-step, and turned to Eric. Her stomach fluttered once again, but she felt unsure of herself.

Eric nearly stumbled into her. "What is it?"

She sighed. "You'll admit there's something going on between us, something strange?"

He nodded.

"I like you but I'm worried," Jen continued, "that we'll do something we may come to regret. I don't want that to happen."

"I understand," Eric said, adjusting his sunglasses that had slipped to the edge of his nose. "Trust me. Just check it out, and if you want to go then I'll bring you right back."

"Okay," she relented and they began to walk again. "What's so important that I have to see this place with you?"

Eric shrugged. "Honestly, I don't know. Something just tells me you have to see it."

A couple of kids on bikes sped by, briefly separating the couple. When they came together again, Eric fumed. "See now, this wouldn't happen in the fall. It's why I liked it way more than summer. You can't even walk down a sidewalk." Jen was used to outbursts like this, what, with living and working in Manhattan. She didn't bat an eye.

They walked back to town along Spring Street passing the Hotel Manisses, and then took a right on Water Street. They separated hands and followed a narrow path that led to a set of stairs. The stairs at first appeared to stand alone in the lot. They looked peaceful and eerie at the same time. It was as if they were built as a stairway to the sky.

Eric went up first. "These stairs," he said as he climbed, "used to lead to the Ocean View Hotel. The grandest hotel on Block Island that burnt to the ground in the mid-1960s."

Jen followed him and saw what the steps really led to. Strewn about were crumbling stone foundations and mysterious pathways that wound around the property. Jen stopped and placed her hand on her chest as she took it all in. The place looked sad and yet familiar. Suddenly, the ground shifted under her feet. She nearly lost her balance, but Eric raced to her side and held her up. When he touched her, the buzzing they initially felt while eating at Finn's returned. Only this time, the ground buzzed as well.

"What is that?" they both said simultaneously.

"It felt like an earthquake," Eric said, "but I've never heard of them happening around here. Not like that, anyway."

A large foundation sat below them, and eroded concrete steps led down into the foundation.

"This," Eric said, gesturing "is where the hotel stood. You can kind of get a feel for the scope of just how big it was." He swept his hands across the expanse. "Now it's been turned into a park." He brought Jennifer over to the pavilion. She walked before him, looking around. Eric leaned against a column and stared out at the ocean waves. "I sometimes come here to write."

She turned back to Eric and saw the center of town behind him. The Harborside and Finn's Seafood were there. She could see people walking in and out of stores. A boat was leaving the harbor and mopeds buzzed around. Jen glanced at the lot and scratched her forehead. "Okay, now I know I've been here before," she said, transfixed by the scene, hypnotized. "Something bad happened here." She thought to herself, 'To me here.' She spoke very deliberately, almost in monotone.

Eric stood by her side, their hands brushing against each other. "Yeah, the Ocean View Hotel was here. It burned to the ground." He paused and scratched his stubbled chin. "Some thirty years ago, back in the late 1960s."

Jen brushed her hand across Eric's shoulder. "Do you come here often?"

"Yes." He smiled. "It seems rather morbid, I guess, but I've been attracted to this place since I was a kid. My friends think it's a bit strange." They exited the pavilion and sat on the grass near top of the nearby bluff. "A place of death. But I don't feel that way," Eric continued. "For me, it's inspiring. I get a sense of renewal when I'm here. Some days, I'll bring my laptop and sit here all day. I get to come out and actually enjoy the island. Bill may be right. Maybe I do spend too much time in front of my computer, but at least I get outside. I'm not stuck in the house while I write. I get to interact with the island…and that's the best part."

Eric peered out at the horizon. "See that?" He indicated the farthest point. "There's a tiny white speck. See? It's moving very slowly."

Jen smiled. "Oh, yeah.," she said, nodding. "What is it?"

Eric looked at his watch. "It's the four o'clock ferry from New London. You'd probably be on it if you were going back today."

"But I'm not," she said, smiling at him. Then she added, "You love the island, don't you?"

"Does it show?"

"Oh, yeah," she said. "Just the way you speak about it. Like the ferry? How many people could pick out a dot on the horizon and tell me what it was? And the way you react to people. Like those bikers before. Hell, that's commonplace in the city all year round. But here, I can tell it isn't." She squeezed his hand. "You're just so protective of the island. It's one of the qualities that makes you so nice to be around. That you care about your home."

Something shifted on the horizon. A blurred image. While Jen was transfixed, Eric shuddered and fell back against the hard-packed earth.

"Did you see that?," Jen said. She looked down to see Eric lying flat on the ground. She knelt over and he reached out. "Oh my God," she said, helping him up. "Are you alright?"

He sat up with some effort. "See what?" Once she knew he was okay, she left out a snort. "It's gone now," she said.

"What was it?" He wanted to know.

Jen frowned. However, even frowning didn't mar her beauty. Her blue eyes sparkled. Her blond hair still shined under that ubiquitous Yankees hat. Feeling unsure of what to say, she shrugged. "I don't know. It was gone too quickly. It was big though, whatever it was."

A cloud passed overhead. Eric stood up and stretched, trying to release the tension that the shock wave produced. His knees buckled and he fell back again.

Jen was there to catch him this time, and she eased him to the ground in her outstretched arms.

"What is it? Is there something you're not telling me? Are you okay?" This time, there was a look of horror on her face.

He shrugged. "I just felt... I don't know... strange. Like something passed through me. A jolt... like my whole body became numb. Nothing like this has ever happened here before." He paused for a moment to catch his breath. "Wow, that was bizarre."

Jen sighed. "Are you sure you're alright?"

"Yeah, positive." He stood up and brushed off his pants. "There," he said, sighing. "I'm fine."

"Do you want to go home? Maybe you need to see a doctor."

"Really, Jen. I appreciate your concern but all I need is your company.

Jen gave him a once over and decided to trust him. "So, what's it like here in the winter?" she asked, changing the subject. "It must get boring?"

"Yeah, sometimes, but you get used to it." He ran his hand through his hair and smiled at her. "It does take a certain kind of person to enjoy the solitude. But I go off island once or twice a month. It helps break up the long winter months." He shifted his feet and stretched his legs a bit, then glanced out at the water. "Island life isn't for everyone. If you're used to a lot of activity, I wouldn't recommend it." He laughed, remembering what happened to Jason and Natalie, a couple he knew. "I have some friends who lived in New York. They thought it would be quaint to sell everything and move here. They didn't even make it to Christmas. By the middle of December, they were gone. We keep in touch and they still have their home here, as a summer home only, but they'll never live here year-round."

"Would you ever consider leaving?"

"The island?" He shook his head. "I doubt it. Over there," he said, "far past the Harborside, is North Light, another one of my favorite places. You probably saw it this morning from the ferry." He grew quiet for a moment, closing his eyes. When he opened them again, he looked at Jen. "My house faces North Light. I don't think I could ever leave permanently, and not have the view each day. I'm an islander, and that'll never change." Taking a breath, he added, "There are things I love and things I don't. Like, right now? This is a good time. I enjoy showing the island to new people. It's almost like I'm seeing it for the first time." He squinted against the sun. "Especially now that I am seeing it with you."

"Oh... something's happ—" His knees buckled again, causing him to fall back and strike his head on the ground. "What the *hell* is going on?" A tingling began at the back of his neck. His body trembled and sweat dripped down his temples and into his eyes. He couldn't get up. It was like a field of energy was pinning him against the ground.

Jen screamed, then yelled out for help to anyone who might be within earshot.

"No," he said. "Don't. You'll only draw attention to yourself."

"But you need help," Jen said, her voice slurring suddenly, as if she were intoxicated. "I... I don't like it here. I want to leave."

She stumbled forward a step or two, trying to get away, but she fell over Eric, landing beside him.

❖ ❖ ❖

A couple stepped up to the veranda and sat down in the porch chairs. They watched boats come and go from Old Harbor. Just then the hotel lobby door opened, and an older woman exited. She sat in the last chair beside the young couple.

"I don't think anyone can ever get tired of this view," the woman said to the young couple.

"I could easily live here," Ellen said.

"Me too," Mike agreed.

"I'm sorry. Where are my manners? I'm Anne Wolf, proprietor of Ocean View."

"Pleasure to meet you. I'm Mike and this is my wife, Ellen.

"We're on our honeymoon," Ellen announced.

"That's wonderful! Congratulations. You're enjoying the island, I hope?"

Mike nodded. "It's so peaceful, like a different way of life. More relaxed than anything we know of. Didn't I tell you it was peaceful, honey?"

Ellen looked lovingly at her new husband with her ocean-blue eyes and smiled. She nodded her head. She turned to Anne and pointed down, off the veranda. "What's that place down there?"

Anne shifted in her seat, becoming more comfortable. "That's the Shamrock Inn. Years ago, it belonged to Nicholas Ball who built this hotel." She looked around the veranda, and a glint came to her eyes. "You should have seen the hotel in its glory days."

"I'll admit it has lost much of its luster," Mike added. He shaded his eyes from the sun and smiled. "This was the place to summer. I never stayed here. It was much too expensive for my folks. Now though..." he said sweeping his hand through his salty hair.

Anne's eighty year-old body creaked as she readjusted in her chair. "You don't mind some company, do you? I hardly ever get to talk about this place anymore." She drew in a breath as she regathered her energy.

"I'd love to hear about the island," Ellen said, shifting her feet around to kick off some sand from her shoes. "It really is a beautiful place."

Anne smiled. "Many people felt that way. Hell, you wouldn't believe some of the people that stayed right here at the Ocean View. I saw one of the old guest registers once. Buffalo Bill Cody, P.T. Barnum, even the Vanderbilts summered here. There's a story, although I can't verify this, but I've heard that the U.S. Supreme court held a session here so the justices wouldn't have to interrupt their vacations."

Ellen whistled. "Wow. That's amazing history.

Anne nodded. "Now... well the old hotel is not what she used to be. Some parts are closed off. Some of the rooms don't even have doors. It's sad really, her best days are behind her. We just can't get the clientele anymore." Anne glanced down at her watch. "I've taken enough of your time. I'd better get back to work. It was real nice talking with you. Congratulations again and I wish you a happy life together."

"Thank you," Mike said. He stood up and held the door to the lobby for her. "We should get going ourselves." He glanced down at his watch. "Supper's soon."

"Supper?" Anne raised her brow. "It's only a quarter to four. Dinner's not till six."

Ellen winked. "There's a lot to do in two hours," she said with a smile.

"I see," Anne said, her face reddening. She turned away then. "Well, you have a good time now." She left the couple sitting on the deck.

Mike and Ellen stayed there for another several moments. "Nice lady," Ellen said. They both stood up and stretched.

Mike scratched his chin. "Maybe later we can take a walk to the inn down there." He motioned to the house at the end of the walk. "I'd like to see what they did to Nicholas Ball's place."

"Mmm, that'd be nice." Ellen reached out and took her husband's hand, and together they walked into the Ocean View. After going to their room, Mike showered while Ellen leafed through one of the magazines in the room. When the shower turned off, she lay back in bed and closed her eyes. Through the open window she heard the pleasant sound of the water lapping the beach outside. "You almost done in there, Mike?" She glanced over at the clock. It was four-thirty.

Off in the distance, she heard a siren. She went to the window to investigate, and noticed smoke and fog crawling across the ground. "Honey?" She went to the bathroom door and knocked. "Something's happening out here." She sniffed at the air and it smelled smoke.

No reply.

She knocked again; this time louder. "Mike? Answer me."

Ellen looked back and saw clouds of smoke creeping under the door from the hallway. "Mike!" she screamed. "The hotel's on fire!"

As the smoke filled the room, tears streamed down Ellen's face as her eyes burned. She coughed, trying to expel the fumes from her lungs. It did no good. She raced through the room trying to reach the window, but the smoke was thick. She didn't see the coffee table in the way, and she fell against it striking her head against the wood end-board of the bed.

Mike stepped out of the bathroom wearing his white terry cloth robe. The smoke filled the room and stung his eyes. He just barely saw Ellen who was slumped on the floor by the bed. When he approached, he saw a bloody gash across her right eye. He stooped down to see if she was still breathing.

She was. Barely.

He went to the window and yelled out. No one came. He went to the door and tried to open it, but the heat had warped it, sticking it in the jamb.

He pounded on the door and screamed at the top of his lungs. Again, no one answered. He ran back to the window and shoved his hand through the screen. Now, how would he get down safely with his young wife? She was unconscious. Perhaps even… no, he wouldn't think that. He couldn't think that. He coughed, trying to release the smoke that had already invaded his lungs. It was no use. He was growing weaker. As he gasped for air, a sense of calm came over him. He took one last look at his wife and lay down beside her.

❖ ❖ ❖

The moon was full, and it cast an iridescent glow over the sleeping couple. Jen woke first. She peered out where it seemed only moments ago the hotel stood engulfed in flames. She rose up on one elbow, the cool ground pressing into her skin. Her dress was up around her thighs. She shoved Eric.

"Mike!" she said. "C'mon. Wake up! Wake up, Mike!"

Tears fell from her eyes.

Eric coughed and rubbed his eyes. When he opened them, he was looking up at his beautiful wife. And then it all came flooding back. As he became more aware, he reached out to Jen, touching her face, her arms, her hands. He looked out at the empty lot. "Ellen, is that really you? Oh my God," he said, reaching to hold Jen close. "Oh Christ! I thought I would never see you again." He put his arms around her and caressed the back of her head. He looked at her, smoothed down her hair, and kissed her cheek. "What if... what if you hadn't come back?" he said, tears streaming down his face. His body shook uncontrollably, but he still held her, afraid to let her go. "What if we hadn't remembered?"

Jen reached to wipe his tears away. When she looked at him, she saw his love in those unforgettable green eyes. "But I am here," she said, "and now I'm never leaving."

They held onto each other for several minutes, while the moon above cast long shadows down the deserted lot. Both were afraid to let the other one go, afraid that by releasing each other, they would disappear as the burning Ocean View had in the 1960s.

❖ ❖ ❖

An hour or so later, they lay entranced, fingers entwined once again. They stared at the moon and back at each other, taking it all in. They talked low, their voices mere whispers in the dark. The crickets lent their song to the newly reunited lovers.

Eric heard the steps creak first. Jen was nearly asleep. "You up there, Eric?" A light flashed across his face. He moved his hand over his eyes, shading the glare. "Bill, Tom?"

"We're comin' in." A warning.

Eric got up, straightened his pants, and pulled Jen to her feet. "We'll be out in a second."

Bill met them halfway, Tom directly behind Bill. "Thank God," Bill said, wrapping his arms around both of them. "Tom called me about forty-five minutes ago and said that Lisa hadn't been able to reach Jen on her cellphone. She called the Spring House three times before she was able to get through to Tom. He told me you left for a walk ten hours ago."

"I knew if there was any where you'd be, it would be here," Tom said. "I still don't understand what you find so fascinating about Ocean View Park. This place gives me the heebie-jeebies."

Jen felt bad. How would she explain all of this to Lisa. She decided she wouldn't even try. Jen hid behind Eric, trying to get out from the light's bright glare. "It's not a creepy place for us, is it?" she whispered to him. Eric took hold of her hand.

Bill pulled himself away from Eric and Jen. "Do you have any idea what time it is?" He shined the light toward the road. Nobody was out.

"Are you still gonna try and tell us the two of you only just met?"

Jen smiled. "Actually, we lied." She reached out to Eric, holding him close once again, refusing to let him go.

Arrivals and Departures

S ean Wolf sat in his favorite spot on the top level of the Block Island Ferry, enjoying the breeze on his face. As was tradition, right after he had parked and bought his ticket, he sprinted to the seat he and his brother had mischievously etched their name into so many years ago. His brother was lucky in the sense that his olive complexion and darker hair meant he got to stay out in the sun longer. Sean hated his own blond hair and pale complexion as a kid, because it meant at a certain point his mother took him below deck. He hated his hair before he realized girls loved it. Still, Sean knew he shouldn't be out in the sun for too long.

Sean had been all around the world, but what he liked about Block Island in particular was the fact that he could go about his business without too much interruption. He knew Mondays were typically slow on the ferry, so he always booked his trips for a Monday so he could remain relatively anonymous. Sean not only made a name for himself in the gaming industry, he was also a social media influencer. Often, he'd be seen with media moguls Richard Branson and Mark Zuckerberg. He was the guy photographed by paparazzi walking down the street with musicians like Phil Collins, Sting, and even Lady Gaga, sharing creative ideas and a coffee from Starbucks.

His brother James Wolf, the silent partner in Sean's dealings, had a taste for wealth too but not the fame. Sean liked to refer to him as his invisible partner. The Wolf brothers amassed a large sum of money, enough to stop working when they reached their late thirties. Once they had lined their bank accounts and purchased one too many stocks, they turned to charitable efforts. Using their last name as their inspiration, they created a line of games that helped protect gray wolves in the Midwest.

Sean had always had a fondness for wolves. He and James agreed that if they could get the message out to farmers that wolves weren't as terrible as they were portrayed, perhaps they could save the majestic animals from unnecessary harm, and possible extinction. One game they produced stemmed from an idea they had come up with as kids. It turned the story of "The Three Little Pigs" on its side. Instead of the wolf being the antagonist, the pigs wound up the aggressors.

Despite helping wolves — and others — through charitable giving, Sean wasn't without his own wants.

Two years after starting the wolf foundation he felt he had put in the work demanded of his conscience, and had properly used his money to help better the world. Now it was *his* time to soar. For him, that meant pursuing something he had long dreamed of. His father flew for the military, and Sean loved the thought of flying. After taking a year's worth of flight lessons, he purchased a Cessna 172 Skyhawk.

Flying, it turned out, was in his genes. He took to it like breathing. Sean admired his father for flying for the military, but it was one thing he could never see himself doing. He loved his father, but he couldn't follow in his footsteps as a military man. Sean was a free spirit and didn't do well with regiment. However, this was something he wanted. Doing something you love always makes doing it seem less like work.

Sean kept his plane at the airport in Chester, Connecticut. There was nothing better than climbing in his plane and flying off to anywhere he wanted. Sometimes as he flew, he still pinched himself.

Sean closed his eyes and thought about the first time he brought his girlfriend Kate flying. Every time he looked over her face lit up with pride. As they flew over Long Island Sound, she commented on how amazing the water looked from up so high, and she marveled at the people who looked like ants swimming back and forth. She said at the time: "Can we fly over Block Island?"

He looked over at her and laughed out loud. "I knew I loved you for a reason," he said as he banked left. "When I'm up here I feel untouchable. You know my Dad flew the P3 Orion for years. Then he joined the Air Force and flew the C-5 Galaxy. He inspired my love of airplanes and wanting to fly."

"You've told me that many times," she yelled over the rumbling of the engine. "You're proud of him, aren't you?"

He nodded. "Look down there." He directed Kate to the water below. The pork chop shaped Block Island came into view. As the made a single large circle above the island he said: "We'll get down there soon. I can't wait to show you around. I know I've been promising that for the last two years, but now that things have finally settled down and I'm completely out of the gaming business, we'll finally have some free time to spend doing what we want."

They turned back and started their return to Connecticut, flying over Long Island Sound again. They flew by Rocky Neck State Park and the railroad tracks on the beach. When they flew over Hammonasset Beach, Sean banked the plane to the right and headed inland toward Chester.

After they were on the ground, Kate let out a whoop. "That was amazing!" She leaned across the seat and kissed him. "You're amazing," she said again. "Thank you for bringing me!"

Sean stepped out first, then then assisted Kate. She looked so beautiful, her red hair shimmering in the sun. "I can't think of anything that makes me happier than being up in the sky with you." Next, he grabbed some cleaning spray and a cloth. Wiping down the plane, he glanced at Kate.

"Gotta do this after every trip," he said. "Otherwise grime builds up." He gave the towel a couple spritzes. "What do you say we plan a week on the island for next June? When I get home, I will call my friend Tom. He owns the Spring House. If you like it there, we can begin looking for places to purchase. Sorry I have been busy with flight school. We should have already taken a trip out."

Kate's face lit up in a smile that wouldn't quit. "I can't wait," she said. "And don't be sorry, Sean. We've both been busy. The important thing is now we have so much more time now. I can't wait to start looking for a house with you!"

From the time Sean turned twelve, he had traveled to Block Island many times, at first, just with his family. Once he turned eighteen, he started going every chance he could. He fell in love with the island from the first time his feet touched the ground, much the same way he fell for Kate four years earlier.

Sean opened his eyes.

The sea breeze suddenly felt like a cold wind. How long had he been daydreaming for? He looked over to Kate - and then realized she wasn't there.

Cancer is such a horrible disease. In some cases, it sneaks up on you and slowly saps your life away. For others, it hits them hard and quick like a fastball hit for a homerun into the "the Green Monster" seats at Fenway Park.

That's what happened to Kate.

One morning she woke up with a headache that wouldn't go away. All that day and into the following, the pain was unrelenting. After the thorough medical exams, the bad news was delivered. Things then went downhill fast. Next thing they knew, Kate was admitted to Smilow Cancer Hospital in New Haven, Connecticut and treatments were started.

Sean stayed with her the entire time, sleeping in the hospital second bed in the room. He paid top dollar — and an extra cash donation to the hospital — to have a double occupancy room turned into a private room for the two of them.

As the cancer continued its ugly march through her body, Kate kept up her resilience as best she could. Some days she didn't appear sick at all. Other days, especially right after a chemo treatment, felt like the end of the world. Kate's pain was Sean's pain, they were that close in mind and spirit. Her once lustrous red hair fell out in clumps; her bright shining eyes were but dull reminders of how she used to shine. She did her best to hide her days of feeling ill. But Sean told her not to put on a brave face for his benefit.

"You don't have to stay with me, Sean," Kate said each time he helped her to bed. "You need to accept that I'm not getting any better. It's time for you to understand that. Promise me you'll accept what happens."

"I promise," he said. "And all the more reason to stay with you now." He sat on the edge of her bed and held her hand. "I'm not going anywhere," he said, wiping tears from his eyes.

It went on like that for a month, then Kate took a turn. The treatments had stopped working. Within a week, she slipped into the place in-between.

Sean couldn't believe what the cancer had done to her. She'd gone from being a bubbly, outgoing woman, in-shape and healthy from her cycling and Cross-Fit classes, to weighing less than ninety pounds. Her voice had grown weak and hoarse. She was just skin and bones. Her last words before she passed were, "Promise me you'll take our trip."

Two weeks to the day after Kate passed, she came to Sean in a dream. "I'm still here with you, Sweetie!" Sean felt her hand caressing his face. "But you have to move on. Remember your promise!"

The dream felt so real he woke with a start, thinking Kate was beside him. On the side of the bed where Kate used to sleep was an indentation at the edge of the mattress like someone had been sitting there and had just stood up. The indentation rebounded slowly, right before his eyes, returning to its normal position. He

ARRIVALS AND DEPARTURES 54

stayed awake the rest of the night, wondering if he had imagined the experience.

And now, here he was in June, six months later, just like they planned, and he was on the ferry boat to Block Island alone, wiping tears from his eyes. He hadn't known he'd been crying until he heard a woman beside him. He was so deep in remembrance he hadn't seen or heard the woman sit down.

"Are you alright?" She touched his shoulder. "I've never known someone to weep while on their way to Block Island. They usually cry when they have to *leave* the island."

He let out a long breath. What should he do? Give the rote answer? The lie? Or should he open up and tell this stranger that he was going through a loss? He opted for the easy answer. "I'm fine."

The woman looked over at him. Eyeing him closely, she said, "No, I don't think you are fine."

Sean ran his fingers through his hair. He then looked away from the woman. "Listen," he said, as gently as he could. "I'm grateful that you stopped to see if I'm okay, but I'm kinda feeling like I need some quiet time. I seriously don't want to offend you."

"Cheryl," the woman said. "Cheryl Ball." She extended her right hand.

"Okay, Cheryl," Sean said, taking her proffered hand. "As I was saying, I really don't want to offend, but I need to be alone."

She shrugged. "Okay. No worries. I don't offend easily." Smiling, she ambled off across the ferry.

Left to his own thoughts once more, Sean reflected on the first time he saw Kate. It was his brother, James, who introduced them. They were sitting in Willoughby's, a local coffee shop, when Kate walked in. To this day, he continued to wonder whether it was a set up. Both James and Kate denied it, but what did it matter. They wound up falling for each other and spent as much time together as possible, starting weekday mornings with a coffee at Willoughby's before each headed to work. The other regulars began calling them "Kasean," first behind their backs, because it seemed they were never apart and displayed such similarity in manner and personality they were like one person.

Then one morning as they strolled in holding hands, Billy, one of Willoughby's regulars, turned and let it slip out into the open when he said, "Oh, look, it's Kasean."

The others in the coffee shop waited for a reaction.

Kate gave a free hearted giggle, and the coffee machines started whirring again.

Kate smiled as she pulled up a chair next to Billy. "Nice moniker. At least you are chivalrous enough to use my name first, Billy Boy."

"It's not Billy Boy, it's Billy T," he corrected. His white hair was cut short and spiked up a bit on the top. Before heading for work, Billy always stopped at

Willoughby's. Billy became friends with Sean and Kate almost immediately upon meeting them.

"I just love to tease you," she said brushing his hair with her hand. Kate was demonstrative that way with everyone. It was one of the reasons she became so accepted at the morning coffee klatch. Everyone loved her. But there was only one she wanted to spend all of her time with. She watched Sean, never taking her eyes off of him as he walked back to the table with her coffee. Half the time, Sean was oblivious to how deeply Kate watched him. They were truly one soul separated at birth.

"So, what are you guys doing today?" Billy T. said. "You going up in your Cessna?"

"Next week." Kate sipped her coffee. "Today we have one more hike, and then we will have done all the land trust property." Hiking was one of their favorite pastimes, as well as walking on the beach and bike riding. Anything active. It's why Sean felt so excited about showing Block Island to Kate. Everything that they both loved to do happened to be at their whim.

"When are you bringing her to Block Island?" Billy said, fixing his hair. "I can't believe you've been dating for four years now, and in all that time together, you haven't brought her to your favorite place. And now that you have your own plane, what excuse do you have?"

"Oh, c'mon guys." Kate sipped her coffee. "Lighten up. It's not just Sean. I've been busy with my work schedule too. We've made plans to go many times but somehow the weather or work interfered. But now, now we've freed up some time in June, and since Sean has left his gaming company, we can finally relax together."

Oh Kate...

❖ ❖ ❖

The tip of Block Island—and the North Light lighthouse that sat upon it—slowly emerged like an oasis in the desert. A melancholy smile came to Sean's face. North Light was his favorite place on the island, and it was always the second location he'd visit on each trip. The first location was Finn's Seafood restaurant—right near the ferry landing in Old Harbor—for a bowl of clam chowder. While the ferry approached the island, he kept ruminating on the loss of Kate, and he could not stop wondering how he was going to get by without his partner in life.

As the ferry rounded Clay Head, Sean spotted the downtown area behind the breakwater harbor, and the ubiquitous white National Hotel in all its pristine glory. As the ferry horn blasted—to warn a pleasure boat out of its path—a chill rolled down his spine. The first genuine smile sprang unconsciously to his face. He was home. The ferry slowly docked, and he saw the people gathered in the parking lot. Kids, adults, dogs on leashes. Because he'd been visiting the island for so long, he was fortunate to have made many close friends there. Many of them were downtown business owners, so he wouldn't lack company if he wanted it.

He kept a car on the island with his friend Tom, at the Spring House. The hotel was just a quarter mile walk from the Old Harbor landing, and he called Tom the night before to let him know he'd be visiting. But his first stop would be Finn's, for that chowder. He walked down the steps from the upper deck of the ferry, his pack on his back. When his feet touched Block Island ground for the first time, he glanced at his arms. Like clockwork… goose bumps!

Cheryl walked up to him. Laughing, she said, "I do that too. Every time I come home I get goose bumps. All over! It's our bodies, our souls, crying out, 'I'm home.'"

Sean smiled. "I'm sorry if I was abrupt earlier. I've had a rough year and didn't realize the emotion returning here today would bring."

She waved a hand. "I meant it before when I said I don't offend easily." She walked off but then turned back. "I hope you find some peace here, Sean Wolf."

He stepped up the two steps onto Finn's deck, and before approaching the service window, he reached into his backpack for sunscreen. He liberally spread some on his legs, arms, and face. Walking to the open window now, he knocked on the wall several times. "Anyone in there? Let's get some service."

A gruff voice on the other side of the screen said, "Hold on! Hold on!" Sean recognized the voice and laughed out loud. "Oh, are you working today Gary? Or do you spend your days off hanging around work?" Gary quipped back. "I might have known it was you. Who else would be so rude?"

Gary walked around the kitchen and stepped outside. He hugged Sean. "Listen," he said. "I heard about Kate. I'm so sorry. I understand how much you wanted to show her the island. Whatever you want today, it's on me." He patted his friend on the back and gave him one more embrace. "I gotta finish up some paperwork and I have a meeting in about ten minutes but call me later. We'll get together."

Gary Mott managed Finn's Seafood. His tousled, light brown hair, and his glasses askew on his face, were signs he needed to take a break. He had about four days' worth of growth on his face as well.

"You look like hell," Sean said. "When did you last get a full night's sleep?"

Scratching the stubble on his chin, Gary said, "What's sleep?" He walked back inside, and turned to the young girl who stood by the window taking orders. "Whatever he wants, Molly," he said pointing to Sean, "it's on me."

Sean ordered the only thing he ever ordered. "A bowl of clam chowder, coleslaw, and a glass of water with lemon, please." Finn's was the only place he ate coleslaw; there was something about the way it was prepared that appealed to him. He chatted with the girl at the window while waiting for his food.

"Have you worked here long?"

"My third season," Molly said. "I take it you're a regular here. On the island, that is."

"Almost an islander. Been coming since I was twelve. Every spring and summer. I'm here now to find a place to buy."

Molly smiled. "This is your lucky day then. My brother's in real estate. I'm sure he can help you." She reached under the counter and dug in her purse. She handed Sean a business card. Ed and Cheryl Ball: Block Island Real Estate. "Call them anytime and tell them I said to take care of you."

When Sean saw the names on the card, he did a double take. "You're kidding me! You know Cheryl Ball?"

"She's my sister-in-law. Why? Do you know her?"

"Not really," Sean said as he swatted at a mosquito. "She was on the ferry with me on the way over this morning."

Molly handed him a tray with his food. "Oh, that's right. I forgot. Cheryl was on her way back today. Weird coincidence that you met her like that."

"Wow. You know, I've never believed in coincidence, Molly. I believe everything is connected. Like a stone on a beach. The stone is not really alone. It's connected to the sand, and the sand is connected to other stones, and everything plays into everything else to make the whole. There's a reason Cheryl stopped to talk with me on the ferry."

"You and my brother will get along just fine." Molly walked back to the kitchen then. "Enjoy your stay. Hope you find a house that works for you. And don't forget to call my brother if you need any help." Sean took his tray, looked for a table in the shade, and sat down. The sidewalks were congested. Sean knew from experience that by the weekend, the population would double, at the least. Fridays in July and August were particularly active. He felt happy knowing he had a few days before the weekend would kick into full swing. Once he finished his food, he returned his tray to the window. He saw Molly standing in the kitchen. "Molly," he called out.

She returned to the window. "Hey, Sean, how was the food?" She smiled.

"Always the best. And I just wanted to say it was nice meeting you and thanks for the info on your brother and Cheryl."

"My pleasure," she smiled.

Sean grabbed his large backpack and started toward his hotel. When he was halfway up Spring Street, he saw the red tiled roof of the Spring House Hotel appear over the crest in the road, the famous white Adirondack chairs lined up on the front lawn facing the ocean. A soft southerly breeze blew in off the water. He strolled up the long driveway, passing the white chairs. He took his time, savoring every step. As he stepped onto the hotel veranda, a young girl with a name tag greeted him. "Good morning. Are you checking or would you like a table on the porch?"

"Actually, I'm here to see Tom."

"Oh. Okay. And you are?"

"Just tell him a dear friend is finally here, please."

She returned a moment later with Tom following behind. "Oh my gosh. I don't believe it," Tom said. "It's good to finally see you." Tom embraced his old friend, his long hair flying all over Sean's face. Pulling away, he said, "I'm so sorry about Kate."

Sean looked away then, covering his sudden surge of emotion. When he turned back, he took in a long breath. "Thanks, Tom. It's hard being here without her, and we planned this trip so many times but never made it happen. I see you haven't changed. Still desperately clinging to our youth." Despite the five-year difference in their ages, Sean being thirty-seven to Tom's forty-two and Sean's slim build to Tom's huskier physique, each man still believed he could take the other down in a brawl.

"Ha-Ha. You're too funny, Sean. This is island life. No one dresses professionally here. Go on. Get outta here." Tom laughed. "I think there's one of your favorite rooms still available. I'll make sure you get it. If there's anything else I can do for you, you know you only need to ask."

"I appreciate that. Right now, I'm just here to get my car. I'll be back a little later. Love you, man." He returned the embrace. "Without you and Bruce, I don't know that I could have survived Kate's loss."

"I'm always here for you, buddy. Back to work for me," Tom said, and Sean walked to his Honda HR-V that was parked behind the hotel.

Next to Tom, Bruce Pigott was Sean's oldest friend on Block Island. Sean's uncle graduated from high school with Bruce. And Bruce was now the head chef at the National Hotel Tap and Grille. When Sean realized his old friend had moved to Block Island along with Tom Norris, the decision to return became that much easier.

Sean drove back downtown and parked in the Old Harbor lot, nearest a small area of beach that few people used. He reached into the back of the SUV and took out his beach chair, which he carried down to the beach and sat near the edge of water. As was his hope, there weren't many people here. It's why Sean liked it. He could sit here and be left alone for the most part. It's also why Block Island appealed to him. He needed a place where he could decompress from the public and Block Island satisfied his need for that. He closed his eyes and rested for a time.

When he opened his eyes, he saw something drift just beyond his peripheral vision, something on the horizon. Something huge and bright. He shut his eyes tight, then shook his head, attempting to clear the phantom image. When he looked again, whatever he had seen was now gone. Glancing at his watch, he decided to return to the Spring House.

As he drove down Spring Street, avoiding pedestrians and bikers, he glanced out the driver's side window at the ocean. He took a deep breath. For the second time today, he couldn't help but feel that smile spread across his face. Sean truly loved it here. As he continued to the Spring House, passing the 1661 Inn on his left, he glanced out the side window again and this time he saw it again. Something materialized on the horizon. Something quite big, judging from the distance. He couldn't quite decide if there was something there, or if his imagination was playing tricks with his sight.

When he blinked, it was gone. What could it have been? He pulled into the Spring House driveway still not quite sure he'd seen anything at all. But that nagging feeling kept returning, like a buzzing mosquito that wouldn't leave until it found its mark. Had he really seen something? Or could it have just been the distress of being here without Kate? Sean opted for that choice and slipped out of his SUV. He pulled his overnight bag out and made his way up the lawn. Walking up the steps to the porch, Sean noticed people outside watching him, nodding to him, and whispering to themselves.

He could only imagine what they were saying. Fortunately, only his closest friends, Tom and Gary, knew about Kate. He didn't know if he'd be able to keep up his carefree facade if he had to retell the story over and over. Sean found it difficult to share his innermost feelings with others, especially strangers. He'd much rather listen to what other people had to say than to divulge his own thoughts. Tom was his oldest friend on the island, and it was challenging enough seeing him after losing Kate.

Sean knew his friends meant well and were only trying to help, but having to share in the pain flooded his thoughts with emotional turmoil. Having so many eyes on him created more stress than he needed.

This is what he hoped to avoid by spending his time here. If he wanted this kind of scrutiny, he could very well have opted for a more public vacation area. Block always appealed to his introversion, especially since becoming a public figure. He walked past the whispering folks, opened the door, and strolled to the front desk.

Tom saw him return, reached under the desk to grab a set of keys, and came out to greet his old friend again.

"So glad you decided not to cancel. Kate would have wanted you to enjoy the island." He handed him his keys. "Did you take your Cessna over?"

"Seriously? You know I love the ferry. Sitting outside on the water is the only way to get here."

Tom nodded. "You're right. Do you need anything else?"

"I think I'm set. Thanks, though."

"You're in your usual room, like I said. Facing the water." You can stay as long as you like, Sean. You know you're welcome here anytime." Tom swept his hair away from his face and drew in a breath. "I have an idea for you," he said. "I know you don't need to work, what with the deal you made on the sale of your business. And I know you're still getting residuals from the games you and James produced." Tom moved closer and in a conspiratorial whisper he said, "What if you helped me manage the place for free room and board? That way we both get what we want? I get some much-needed help from someone I trust implicitly, and who knows how to run a business right, and you get a place to stay."

Hmmm, Sean thought. This is why he loved it here. Those who knew him took care of him. "I like it," he said.

"Great! By the way, I made sure to put the bed genie in for you."

Since Kate's time at Smilow, he'd found himself unable to sleep lying prone. He'd spent so much time sleeping in a hospital bed that he found it near impossible to sleep unless his head was raised. Part of it, he knew, was psychological. With the head of his bed raised at home he could freely imagine he still slept in the hospital room with Kate. But he also found he got a better night's sleep with his head propped up.

He went to his room and paused for a moment to look out at the ocean. Then he decided a walk is what he needed. His visit to North Light would have to wait. He just couldn't go there yet, not with Kate being so fresh in his thoughts.

He thought about Southeast Light and headed there instead. He walked out the front door and again found himself scrutinized by those people sitting on the front porch. Taking in a breath, he thought about how he wished he could avoid those faces. His feet carried him off the steps and onto the lawn. His head had other plans, and he turned back. Even though he didn't know these people, he decided to put an end to their stares.

He stepped back on the porch and smiled at everyone.

"Hello everyone. Yes, I'm Sean Wolf. I understand your curiosity, and I don't blame you. I can take a guess that because you've only ever seen hyped-up news reports about me that you probably think I have everything a person could possibly want in life."

Sean kept smiling as he spoke. Some on the deck nodded and smiled along with him.

"But let me tell you something." Sean pulled one of the iron outdoor dining chairs away from a table, and sat down backward in the chair. "I've been coming to Block Island for over half my life. It's been my sanctuary, the place I go to re-center." He paused, wondering whether to continue. He wondered if telling these strangers what happened to him and why he needed this sanctuary more now than ever would help or hinder his well-being. The small group of women and men moved closer. They clearly wanted to hear what came next.

One of the women said, "I can see you're feeling distressed Mr. Wolf. Block Island has always been a restorative place for me too." She was an older woman, late sixties probably, with short gray hair. "I'm Sarah by the way."

He nodded to her, shuffled his feet a bit, and pondered whether he should continue sharing his truth.

Standing behind the group was Tom with a big smile on his face. Shaking his head, he said "For someone who professes to value his privacy, you certainly seem to be relishing this attention. I thought you were on your way to Southeast Light."

"I am. I mean… I mean I was. I just got caught up here."

"Uh-huh." Tom looked away from his friend. "Keep telling yourself that, Sean. Maybe you can convince yourself. But you and I know that's not true." Tom exited the porch into the lobby, closing the door behind him.

The diversion provided Sean with the necessary time to make a decision about how much further he wanted to go. Without discussing what really brought him to the island this time, Sean ran the chance of becoming a whispering campaign again. "Tom's right," he finally said. "Generally, I'm not comfortable discussing the personal challenges I'm facing. I'd rather work these out on my own. Despite being a media darling, I am a very private person. It's why Block Island appeals to me. Even though it's small compared to other resort islands, and the percentage of acres to people is smaller, I've always felt like we respect each other more."

More nods and smiles graced the crowd.

"This is a particularly difficult time for me at the moment." Sean swallowed hard and took in a deep breath. "This trip was supposed to be a celebration. My girlfriend and I were supposed to be looking for a place on the island to buy." He paused again. "She's gone now. Cancer. She had never stepped foot on the island, only saw it once from above, from an airplane, but we had these marvelous plans to live here, and I couldn't wait to share with her why I feel such an affinity for Block Island. Now that's impossible. It wasn't meant to be."

Sarah stepped close and reached for his hand. He gave it willingly. "I'm so sorry," she said. "My husband and I have been coming to the island all our lives, so we understand how you feel. I'm so sorry you can't share that with your girlfriend."

"Thank you. This place has meant so much to me for so long. And now I can't share it with my best friend. So, you see, everyone has a secret. We have to learn to stop judging people only by what we think we know. There's always more that we don't know. And the sad part is, we both could have been here much earlier in our relationship. We were together for four years. And we never made the time to get her out here." He gulped in a sob. "Four years!" Sean sat there and stared out at the fresh green lawn and the ocean beyond that. Weeping inside, he could only think about what could have been. As he continued to gaze into the distance, something formed out on the ocean. It was that same "thing" that appeared earlier when driving to the hotel. Becoming agitated, he started to tremble. "Look! Tell me you see that..." he said to the crowd, directing their attentive faces to the horizon.

"See what?" one of them asked.

Sean stepped off the porch and again focused on the ocean in front of him. Whatever had started to form out on the water had vanished just as quickly. Why could only *he* see this? Now he wasn't so sure he was up for a walk to Southeast Light. He stood on the front lawn looking back at the people on the porch and then looked out at the ocean again. "You really didn't see anything?" he asked.

"Nope," they all said. "Are you alright?"

"Yes. I mean..." It was the third time Sean had seen something emerge off the coast, then vanish. He couldn't help but remember the adage: Once is an accident, twice is a trend, and three times is a pattern. He glanced back at the ocean horizon. "I think I need that walk after all," he mumbled to himself and left the group standing on the porch — most of them looking befuddled — and started walking across the hotel lawn toward the road that would take him to Southeast Light.

When he reached the road, he picked up his pace, and he thought about what his brother James had advised. In order to move on and stop feeling sorry for himself, James suggested that he might feel better if he talked about Kate and what she had meant to him. He then thought about the people he'd left standing on the porch.

"You can't keep everything bottled up," James had said numerous times. "Kate wouldn't want that. And just look at what it's doing to you in. She loved you, Sean. She would want you to keep her memory alive, but talking about her. Not by locking it away. Not by keeping her from the world like she had never existed. The only way *out* is *through*. You know that!"

He shook free of the thoughts and glanced back at the Spring House a final time. One of the women on the porch waved at him. He waved back and then headed to the light house. What if James is right? he thought while keeping his brisk pace. Maybe I do keep too much inside. I did start to feel better after being honest, even if it was with a bunch of strangers.

There were several bands of traffic on the road, groups of walkers, and here and there singles. And of course, the omnipresent mopeds and bicycles. A typical summer day on Block Island: hot, crowded, and crazy. Sean didn't care though. As Cheryl Ball had said when she stepped off the ferry that morning, "This is home."

In the distance, he saw Saint Andrew's Parish Center, and he suddenly felt compelled to turn and look out at the ocean. In that moment, he watched as the same mirage he imagined several times before began to appear once again. This time he saw it fully form. Three wooden masts appeared momentarily, and then just as quickly the clear for of a tall ship vanished. He stopped in the middle of the road and shut his eyes hoping that when he opened them again, he'd see only the vast empty horizon.

His thoughts were interrupted by a young woman who bumped into him from behind. He turned in surprise and opened his eyes to look at her. Three young men stood with her.

"What's going on?" one of the fellows said.

Sean did not answer, but instead turned away and looked back out to the ocean. The site of the tall ship slowly merged back into the horizon. "Don't you see that!?"

"See what? There's nothing out there."

The apparition had melted entirely back into the sea.

The group stepped around Sean and continued walking in the direction of Southeast Light.

"The lighthouse is just another five minutes from here," said one of the young men in the group, was they walked on. Before they were out of earshot the young woman said, "Hey guys, I think that was Sean Wolf we just bumped into."

"No way," said one of them. "I heard he hasn't been to the island in like four years."

Their voices faded off, leaving Sean to contemplate about what he thought he saw on the ocean. Logic dictated only be one thing: apply Occam's Razor. He then ignored his own instincts and chased the thought from his mind. "No. there *has* to be another explanation," he said out loud as he continued to the lighthouse.

Try as he might, he couldn't shake the feeling that something was changing inside his very being; or had *already* changed inside him. He'd become aware of the etheric, more sensitive side of life ever since Kate's death. This mirage was only the latest example. There was the time just weeks after Kate's passing when he heard her voice, and felt her hand on his face. Something had definitely shifted in him. Determined to discover what was happening, Sean decided to embrace this new feeling. He could no longer hide. James was right: the only way *out* was *through*.

He arrived at Southeast Light and ran into the young woman and three guys that had bumped into him on the road. Without hesitation he approached them.

"Listen," he said. "I'm glad I ran across you again. I want to apologize for stopping so abruptly in the middle of the road, and tripping you up."

"It's alright. I'm Tim. These are my friends Jason, Julie, and Chris," Tim said, indicating the others. "You're Sean Wolf, right?"

He nodded. "So, I've been told," he said with a weak smile.

"I think Chris loves wolves almost as much as you do," Tim said, nodding at the guy with the camera in his hands who had continued walking toward the lighthouse. "The four of us do our best to get here as often as possible. It's our favorite place."

Julie swept a strand of errant hair from her face. "By the way," she said, "I just want to tell you that we're all so inspired by what you do to help endangered wolves. You've done a great service."

"Well, thank you. Just doing what I can. Nice chatting. Enjoy your stay." Sean strolled away then. He walked to the far end of the property and sat near the boulder that marked where the lighthouse had stood before it was moved. He knelt before the boulder, closed his eyes, and rested his forehead against the rock. He smiled again. Block Island: there was nowhere else he felt so relaxed. If he wasn't careful, he'd be asleep in a matter of minutes. As long as he was on Block Island, even the hardest of rocks would make a fine mattress.

As he became sleepier, he heard a woman's voice whisper in his head: "Believe what you're seeing" the voice said. The words were as clear in his ears as the ringing of a ship's bell.

He jerked his eyes open. "Kate?" He leapt to his feet. Brushing the sand from his pants, he looked around and saw several people staring at him. "I'm alright," he said, smiling. As he walked away, embarrassed for the moment, he thought again about Kate's visit — in voice and in thought—after she died. And now here on Block Island, he had experienced these unexplained events: the latest being the whispering female voice. What was it she said? "Believe what you're seeing?" What exactly was he seeing? As he made the long walk back to the Spring House, Sean decided he could no longer keep these paranormal incidents to himself.

He was thankful that his mind was clear on the walk back to the hotel, and that no more visions haunted him. Once he reached the hotel lobby, he walked straight to Tom's office, behind the front desk. "Knock, knock," he said. "Can we talk?" Sean took the empty chair in front of Tom's desk.

Tom raised his head, looking away from his paperwork. "What's up?"

Sean eyes darted around the small office. "Can we go somewhere where we won't be interrupted?"

Tom walked around the desk, closed the door, and put a hand on his Sean's shoulder. "When that door is closed everyone knows I'm not to be disturbed." Tom sat behind the desk and looked at his friend. "Now tell me what's going on?"

Sean rose from the chair and paced the small office, glancing out the window in the wall behind Tom. He swept a hand through his hair, cleared his throat, and took a deep breath.

"When I was walking past Saint Andrew's Parish, on my way to Southeast Light, I saw something out on the ocean. It caused me to stop dead in the middle of the road, and a group of four people nearly knocked me to the ground. I saw it a few times earlier too: on my walk up here from the ferry landing, and when I was on the front porch addressing that crowd. And each time I see it, and it looks like it's trying to fully form into whatever object it's trying to become, it immediately vanishes. Kind of like… like how when you come out of a vivid dream you lose all the detail when you finally come fully awake."

"Maybe they are dreams."

"Who dreams when awake."

"Daydreams, I meant. Moments of escape your mind is fabricating. I know you're dealing with your intense grief for Kate. The mind will find a way to protect itself."

"It's not daydreams. The visions are too vivid. Brief, yes, but very vivid. As in *real*."

"Okay, did these people other people — your fans on the porch or the group in front of St. Ann's — see what you saw?" Tom walked back to his desk and sat down again.

"They said they didn't. And now that I'm here with you, I'm beginning to wonder whether I really did see anything except for…" Sean looked away from his friend and glanced out the window again.

"Except for what?"

Sean took a deep breath. "When I arrived at Southeast Light, I walked back to the marker boulder where the lighthouse used to stand. I knelt down against the boulder and closed my eyes. I felt immediately relaxed, as I always do out here, and I must have dozed off for a moment because I swear, I heard Kate. You know it's not the first time that's happened. Remember when I told you that two weeks after she passed, I felt her presence, like she visited me, and sat on the edge of the bed?"

"Yes. Go on," Tom said.

"So, just as I dozed off against the boulder, I heard Kate say, 'Believe what you're seeing.'"

"What do you think you're seeing?"

Sean shrugged. "I have no idea." He shuddered then, almost as if keeping a tsunami at bay.

"C'mon, Sean. You know that's not true. You surely do have some inclination. You wouldn't be in my office talking about this if you didn't. How long have we been friends? I've known you well before Kate. I've known you before you started flying. I've known you since you started coming to Block Island on your own. Tell me what's happening. I know there's something else. I can feel it, Sean. It's right there between us."

Another tremor. Then everything came to the surface. Sean broke down. "I miss her, Tom!" His body trembled. Wracked with grief, he fell into the chair he'd been sitting in earlier. His head in his hands, he convulsed, his entire body shaking as if it had a mind of its own. His chair rocked back and forth in concert with the convulsions his body went through as he wept out loud. When the tide broke, he looked up Tom and breathed in deeply. "How... how can I enjoy being here without... without Kate? This was supposed to be our time."

Tom sat by and let him go on. "I bet you haven't done this in all the time she's been gone."

Sean shook his head, doing his best to regain his composure. Still shuddering from the aftershocks, Sean slowly returned to a semblance of human. He took another long deep breath, he released it, and felt like he could smile again. He raised his head. "I'm sorry I lost it."

"You're sorry? What are you sorry for?" Tom shook his head. "You've got nothing to apologize for. That was long overdue, Sean. I'm happy you came to me. I bet you feel better now."

Sean wiped the last tears from his eyes. "I do. And you were right earlier too, when I spoke with your other guests. James always told me the only way out is through. I'm understanding that now."

Tom chuckled. "Smart guy, that James. So," he said, adjusting his feet under the desk. "What do you think Kate meant when she said, 'Believe what you're seeing'?"

"So, you think it was Kate?"

Rolling his eyes, Tom let out an exasperated breath. "Of course, I do. And you do too. You've said it yourself. Everything that's happening is related to Kate. In fact, I'd be willing to bet that what you've been experiencing since arriving here is tied to her. What do you think you saw? And don't tell me you have no idea."

Still unable to say, Tom interjected. "You know what I think? I think it's the Princess Augusta." He waited for Sean's response. When none was forthcoming, he counted off the times Sean said he had seen something. and where. "You do understand of course, that where you've seen whatever it is you've seen, that's in the area where that ship ran aground?"

Sean got up again and started pacing the office. "Yes, Tom. I know that. It's not the right time of year and not even the right time of day. It's called The Palatine Lights for a reason. Lights generally appear when it's dark."

Tom watched and waited to see if his friend would piece the puzzle together. He decided not to help him. He eyed Sean, willing him to see the connection. It was all to no avail.

"What?" Sean said.

Shaking his head, Tom said, "Nothing."

"Alright. Two can play that game." Sean laughed out loud. "We've known each other for over twenty years, Tom. As you said earlier, we can read each other all too well. I can't compel you to tell me what you're thinking."

"What have you always said about that, Sean? That you find it so much more gratifying when you solve a challenge on your own. Remember all those times you'd call me from Connecticut and complain about a glitch in one of your games? I'd listen and offer advice to help you see the end result. Not give you the answer, but push you in the right direction? You have all the pieces, now you only have to arrange them to see the big picture. Here. I'll even lay out what you've said. Kate told you to believe what you're seeing. It's not the right time of year you said. It's not even the right time of day. Palatine Lights appear when it's dark." Tom smiled here. "That's all I'm saying. The rest is up to you. Now I've got work to do and so do you."

Sean walked to the door. "You're rotten, Tom," he said, laughing. As he moved around the front desk, he realized he hadn't eaten since lunch and was starting to feel hungry. The National was calling his name. Walk or drive? Just a ten-minute walk, and he wouldn't have to park. On his way there, he puzzled over what Tom had said. Of course, he was right - he could trust Tom. Sean just wanted to know what his friend had been thinking. He also understood that if Tom told him, he'd be leading Sean to the truth. He wanted Sean to come to the truth on his own. It was yet another reason they were so compatible. They both helped each other without giving the easy answers they were searching for.

He climbed the steps to the National Hotel and waited for a host to show him to a table. "One?" the host asked.

Sean nodded.

"Right this way." He was guided to a table at the end of the porch. "Your waitress will be here shortly. Enjoy your dinner."

Sean loved coming to the National. He had a clear view of the Atlantic Ocean in front of him, beyond the breakwater ferry boat harbor. He could watch the ferries as they traveled back and forth from the harbor to their home port in Galilee, Rhode Island. Below him, he watched people dart in and out of stores.

The waitress came and held out a menu. Sean waved it away. "I'm going to have mahi mahi, asparagus, and a glass of water with lemon. Please tell Bruce to grill the mahi medium-well."

The waitress nodded. "You know Bruce?"

"I helped him get the head chef position at the Saybrook Fish House in Connecticut years ago."

"Really?" she said. "He's told me about that place. It was his first head chef job. I'll get your order in."

Once his food arrived, Sean looked out at the water. The five o'clock slow ferry to Galilee sat at the dock, abuzz with passengers beginning to board and the cars lined up in the parking lot, ready to be boarded. He thought about all those people having to leave the island and head home, which was always the very worst about the island: the leaving. Every time he boarded the ferry to head back to the mainland, a pit formed in his stomach and a whole in his heart when he realized his time on this paradise had once again come to an end. It was the paramount reason he and Kate talked about finding their own place here, so they would not have to leave unless for a rare good reason.

He returned his gaze to the empty chair on the other side of the small table, and felt a darkness settle over him. Oh, Kate, he thought as he started eating. You would have loved it here. How am I supposed to find a house without you? And even if I do find a house, without you, Kate, it will never be a *home*. He went back to his plate and continued eating, without any joy. He pushed the plate away when he finished.

He sat back in the chair. His body was now satiated, but his spirit felt empty. A few moments later, his waitress returned, picked up his plate, and left the bill after he refused dessert. "Bruce said he wishes he could come out and say hello, but we're jammed tonight. He said to call him soon."

"Sure. Thank you." Drawing in a breath and slowly releasing it, Sean watched the waitress leave, not really hearing himself answer. He stretched his stiff legs under the table, and then looked out to the ocean horizon. Just then, the form—like before—began to appear out of thin air. He closed his eyes, and thought, "Not again." When he opened them, there it was, the tall ship, slowly drifting towards Southeast Light. This time, the wooden ship was fully formed, three masts with sails flapping in a slight breeze. Everyone else in town and those eating here on the porch were oblivious to the ship as it sailed closer to the island than at any time before. The boat sailed proudly, in full sails, past

Old Harbor, heading South. He hurriedly left the cash for his bill along with a hefty tip. Referring to the wooden ship out on the water, he said to anyone who would listen, "Does anyone see that old sailing ship out there, just south of the harbor?" Those eating nearby looked to where he directed them. No one seemed to indicate that they saw anything and all went back to their meals.

Sean raced down the porch stairs to the sidewalk and ran down Water Street to getting closer to the sailing ship. The ship continued its slow, inexorable journey to its demise. In his head, he heard Kate's voice.

"It's time, Sean."

Time for what?

No answer was forthcoming as he followed the ship on foot, passing crowds of people strolling in and out of downtown shops and pubs, no one paying any attention to the ship out on the water.

"How can no one see it?" he said aloud.

Kate echoed in his mind. "Believe what you're seeing."

He didn't know if he actually heard her anew or if he remembered her voice speaking that phrase from earlier.

"It's time, Sean."

He clearly heard that.

Time for what? His feet carried the full length of Water Street, and then up the Spring Street hill toward the Spring House hotel. Dusk began to settle over the island, and he continued running, passed the hotel, passed Saint Andrew's Parish. Not really understanding what was happening, Sean followed where he was being led, trailing the Princess Augusta as she continued her trek southward, parallel to the island's eastern shoreline.

Now convinced that the ship he pursued on foot was indeed the Palatine, he had no clue why no one else saw it or why he was the one person chosen to see it. He thought back to his conversation with Tom, attempting to make sense of this crazy event that seemed to be happening to him and him alone.

What had Tom said? That the Palatine light appeared when it was dark? Tom said it like Sean should be naturally aware of something.

He passed the plaque that noted where the Princess Augusta ran aground. Then, as if guided by an unknown hand, he made his way to the beach.

Kate materialized out of the mist, walking off the burning Princess Augusta as the vessel foundered against the rocks, the flames dancing around her but not engulfing her. Kate reached out with both arms when she arrived on shore. "It's time, Sean," she said again.

Sean backed away, fearful of the apparition before him on the beach. Trembling, he wanted to welcome her outstretched arms and embrace the one person he would ever love the most. Yet another part of him felt afraid.

Kate moved closer, her feet leaving impressions in the sand as she continued to walk forward. She saw Sean looking at the sand as it compressed under her feet. She smiled then, teeth gleaming in the twilight. She stepped closer yet again and reached out to touch him. Flesh meeting flesh.

"How?"

"Shhhh." She put an index finger to his lips. Kate took him in her embrace. Pulling back and gazing into his eyes, she said. "It's time." Salty tears streamed down his face. She moved to wipe them away. "It's time to let me go, Sean. You have to move on without me." She hugged him closer one final time, then released him, and pushed him away.

He collapsed on the sand and watched as she floated back over the water, back to the burning Princess Augusta, away, away from him as he knelt on the wet sand, his arms still reaching, his heart still wanting. "Wait!" he called out.

She stopped her retreat and looked back.

"Why the Palatine?"

"It brought you here, didn't it? The darkness you couldn't release? That's what brought the light to you."

His arms dropped to his sides as more tears fell from his eyes.

Kate then drifted closer, moving back over the water toward him. "That's why you've always been fascinated by North Light and Southeast Light," she said, as he knelt frozen in place on the beach, listening. "It's the light that will always lead you out of the darkness. The only way out is *through*. It's the Palatine Light that guided you. There's so much light within you, Sean. So many people see it. But you don't see it in yourself. Share that goodness in you with the living Sean, the dead no longer need your inner light."

He took in a long breath and wiped tears from his eyes as Kate came back to stand on the shore once again, her feet not touching the sand this time.

"I don't want you to go," he said. "It's so easy to talk to you, Kate. I can tell you anything and I know you won't judge me."

"I understand, Sean. But you have to learn that I'm not the only person in your life. You have to let others see your light too." She moved close, still floating. Touching his face, she said, "And you have to let go of the darkness that holds your soul. The darkness will kill you before you die, and everything good around you will shrivel away. That's not what life is meant to be. You have *life*, Sean. That is the most precious gift the universe has to offer. Cherish it, and share it with others who live too. And always remember I love you, Sean. But don't let my love prevent you from loving again. Let others back into your life." She kissed him gently on the lips and floated away again. "I love you."

Those were the last words he heard, as Kate floated back to the ship and melted away into the eternal flames of the Princess Augusta.

The flames rose high over the ships' masts, making it into a bright, glowing ball. Sean could smell smoke for the first time. He heard voices from above and behind him. He turned around to see dozens of people on the bluff pointing down to the beach.

Someone shouted, "There's a ship burning!" Just as the words left his mouth, the burning ship faded into the twilight, leaving nothing behind but a burning memory in all who were witness.

Sean looked forlornly back to where Kate had been only moments earlier and whispered into the ether, "I love you too." He rose off the sand and brushed himself off.

Some of the onlookers tossed questions out to him as he climbed up the embankment.

"What happened down there?"

"Did the ship sink?"

"Who were you talking to?"

Sean didn't answer. He made his way back to the Spring House, feeling pensive. Kate was right. He did have to let her go. Seeing the Princess Augusta was the only way for him to understand. He would always love Kate. But now Block Island would hold another chapter for him, the one that told the story of how Sean Wolf became a spiritually free man, and learned to love again.

Mad Maggie

Heather Littlefield drove by Southeast Light on her way to work at the National Hotel on a day that should be like any other, but this one wasn't.

She had driven by Southeast Light more times than she could remember, but this time something seemed different about the lighthouse, something she couldn't quite figure out as she drove on, glancing at the lighthouse in her review mirror. Not until she was parked downtown, next to the National, did she realize what appeared unusual.

Unfortunately, she didn't have time to drive back to verify her suspicions. It would have to wait until after work. But she swore that the lighthouse was located farther back from the road than it had been the day before, as if… as if it *now* stood in its original position, before the Block Island

Southeast Lighthouse Foundation moved it away from the eroding bluff back in 1993.

How could that be?

"Was I seeing things? Well, no use overthinking it Heather," she said loud to herself. "I have to impress my new boss today." She stepped out of her Jeep and walked around to the front of the National.

Bruce's friend, Sean Wolf, happened to be standing at the top of the stairs, looking out over the breakwater harbor. With his too-blond hair, piercing blue eyes, and a sweet melancholy smile, Heather had been infatuated with him since she started working there. He and Bruce had been friends for years and on more than one occasion Bruce mentioned how his friend helped him get his first chef job at the Saybrook Fish House in Connecticut.

Sean knew Bruce long before Heather did, having been introduced to him by his uncle. He and Sean's uncle graduated together. It wasn't until he landed a position as head chef at the National that Heather met him.

Sean and Heather had been circling each other for as long as Heather had worked there, hence the familiarity. She felt a connection to Sean, and it wasn't until just recently, however, that she explored the possibility of a relationship with him. She finally set aside her fear of rejection and began openly talking to Bruce about her feelings. It was a testament to the relationship that Heather felt comfortable to talk to

Bruce about this. They'd been friends for so long. Nothing felt off limits.

She'd heard how Sean had lost his girlfriend to cancer some time ago, and that he'd come to the island to find solace. He'd been staying at the Spring House helping Tom, one of Sean's oldest friends, manage the place on a need-be basis.

"Heather," Sean said as he stepped aside to let her pass.

"Mm-hmm." She dug in her purse for her keys. "Bruce isn't here yet."

"Yeah, I know. It's actually you I'm here to see."

Uh oh, she thought, dropping her keys. Her heart raced a bit as she bent down to retrieve them, her shoulder length auburn hair flying in her face. She brushed it aside as she stood, and wondered if Bruce had talk to him? Even though she eventually expected to have this conversation, she still got flustered at the anticipation of it. When she turned to fully face Sean, a strand of hair flopped back into her eye. She swept it aside again and fumbled for the right key on the ring, and then locked the door. Swinging the door open, she said, "C'mon in, Sean. We can talk while I prepare the kitchen."

Once inside, she went to the closet and grabbed a fresh hair net and bunched her hair up inside. Now or never, she thought. She took a deep breath and let it out. "So, what's up?" Heather asked, smiling at him while she pulled on her white chef's coat.

That smile, along with those sparkling green eyes and red hair, hypnotized him. He shook free and thought he shouldn't be feeling this way after so recently losing Kate. He tried to shove those feelings aside, but every time he looked at Heather they returned. Even in her chef's coat, Sean felt she was beautiful.

She pulled lettuce, tomatoes, cucumbers, and carrots from the refrigerator and placed them on the stainless-steel counter. Next, she grabbed a dicing knife and started to dice up the ingredients on an acrylic cutting board. Anything to take her mind off of what would be an awkward conversation — a conversation she wanted to have, nonetheless.

Behind her, Sean helped by rolling silver into the cloth napkins. "You know Bruce and I have been friends for a long time," he said. "He looks out for me."

Uh oh, Heather thought again. Here it comes. She braced herself against the counter near the dishwasher. "I know how that feels. Bruce has been a longtime friend to me as well. But then I suppose you know that."

Sean nodded. "You're right. Anyway, the other night after I stopped by to grab some dinner, Bruce took a break from the kitchen to tell me that you wanted to talk me."

She stepped away from the counter. "He didn't tell you why?"

"Nope. Just that you wanted to talk."

Bless him, she thought. Bruce had her back just like always. Now she had a decision to make. The thought of Bruce going out on a limb for her made this either easy or challenging. She took the challenging path. "Listen," she said. "I know you lost your girlfriend a while ago... and I know you came here to recuperate from that." She paused here for a moment, taking in a deep breath, then plunged ahead. "I've been thinking about you since the first time I met you." She looked away, hiding her blushing face. When she turned back to him, her heart pounded so loudly she could hear it and she was sure Sean could hear it too. She pushed ahead, ignoring the stress. "I'm... I'm usually not so forward, and it generally takes something to push me."

"Mm-hmm. I've been thinking about you too," he cut her off. "Heck, I see you all the time here. How could I not think about you?" He smiled before continuing. "I'm not sure I'm ready to start anything quite yet. Although one thing I remember Kate saying before she passed is that she'll always love me, but not to let her love keep me from opening up again."

Heather nodded. She flushed and her heart raced. Looking away, she stuck her hands in her chef coat and balled them into fists. Letting out a long breath, she gathered her strength and smiled. "You're... you're right. And Kate's right. I... I'm not... I'm not looking to... to create something here that I don't think has the possibility of a future. Am I... am I wrong to feel that you feel something as well?"

"I'm glad you told me. And you're right. I do feel the connection with us." Sean paused here for a moment. He brushed his hand through his hair. Intertwining his hands and separating them again, he glanced at Heather. "I'd be happy to spend time with you, Heather." He waved his hands between the two of them. "You know where I'm staying. Let's grab lunch soon." He approached her and gave her a light kiss on the cheek. "I'll let you get back to work. Tell Bruce I said hello." He turned to leave, then looked back. "Hey," he said. "Why not stop by after work today? Maybe I can get a late dinner for us." He recited his phone number while Heather put it in her phone. "Text me when you leave work."

"I will," she said, smiling. She gave Sean her phone number as well. "See ya a little later."

After he left, Heather smiled. That wasn't so bad, she thought. She returned to prepping the vegetables, forgetting all about Southeast Light.

Bruce walked in several minutes later. "Morning, Heather. Did I see Sean's car outside?" Typical of Bruce, he arrived with the usual smile and not a dark brown hair out of place. Like Tom, Bruce was built like a tank: stout and rigorous. He did his best to maintain a healthy diet. Fish, chicken, and vegetables were his staples.

"I assume Sean stopped by, and from that smile I'm guessing it went well?"

"Yeah, he stopped by. Thank you for telling him I wanted to talk and for not saying why. I so appreciate that. And yes, it went well indeed."

"That's great. I'm so happy to hear that. Sean needs to find some joy. I think you're just the person to bring him out of his shell. Besides, you know me. I always pay my debts, Heather. You've helped me so many times. This is the least I can do."

"Thanks Bruce. Well..." she said, wiping her hand on her apron and looking around the kitchen. "I got here early and stated the salad stations. I just started the ovens so we can get the appetizers going."

She smiled, then retrieved the baking sheets from under the counter. When Bruce set about his tasks, Heather thought about how close she was to Bruce. There were so many times during their friendship where they both shared things with each other they wouldn't dream of telling anyone else. That's how relaxed they felt around each other. They were friends first, which may have seemed odd since they were now colleagues. Sometimes the line blurred. But neither one ever fully crossed it. Theirs was strictly and always platonic. Heather helped Bruce through some particularly difficult situations in the past. Break-ups, staff infighting, financial stress. Nothing was off limits except... that.

One particular time stood out. Bruce arrived at the National an hour earlier than usual and beat Heather in that morning. When she arrived, she heard banging in the kitchen, almost as if someone was throwing things around. As she turned the corner, she caught Bruce smashing a plate. He reached for another and almost let it fly from his hand when Heather walked over.

She knew Bruce's girlfriend of several years, Grace, had thought about breaking up with him on multiple occasions but then they seemed to be doing better. From this outburst, Heather figured things had taken a turn for the worse. "What's happened?"

"I thought we were working things out," he said, collapsing to the floor. "I went home last night, brought Grace her favorite meal." He shuddered and wrapped his knees to his chest. He looked up at Heather and took in a breath. "I called out to her as I walked through the house and made my way upstairs." His voice cracked as he tried to hold back the floodgates. Next, he burst into tears and cried out while rocking back and forth. "I... I went into the bedroom and I... and I saw..." he couldn't get the word out. He reached out to Heather. "She had a man in bed with her. I don't understand. I would never dream of doing anything like that. How could she? Two days before..." He paused between a couple of sobs. "Grace told me she'd never been happier. She said... she said she loved me more every day. I don't... I don't understand it."

Heather knelt beside him. "That's horrible." She wrapped her arms around him, and they sat on the floor like that until one of the secondary cooks arrived. Heather heard footsteps approaching and saw Jim before Bruce noticed and waved him away. "Take some time off," she suggested to Bruce. "You need time to off. I can certainly handle the kitchen."

"No." He stood up, brushing his pants. "If I leave, I'll only dwell on it. This is the best place for me to be." He squeezed Heather's shoulder. "Thank you for being you."

That happened two years ago, and it brought them closer. You'd think it would have turned him off to relationships. Quite the opposite, however. He loved seeing other people thrive. It's another reason he wanted to help Sean and Heather.

It was then that she remembered Southeast Light. "Hey, did you come down Spring Street today?"

"I did. Why?

"Did you notice anything different about Southeast Light? Anything unusual?" She asked while continuing with preparing the appetizers.

He shook his head. Bruce reached for a screwdriver and started to remove the covering from the stove. "I've been meaning to fix that bad burned for a while. No time like the present." A few more screws came out and he popped the covering off. "Just what I thought, a loose wire." He tightened it back onto the coil and put the cover back on.

When Heather was not forthcoming Bruce prodded. "What did you see that was so unusual?"

"When I drove past, something didn't seem right. It seemed like the light house was back in its original place, closer to the bluff."

He glanced over at her. "That can't be." He returned his attention back to the stove, tightening the remaining screws of the cover. "You must have been imagining it. A lighthouse doesn't just up and move on its own."

"I've heard Southeast Light is haunted," she said, finishing the spread of appetizers. "An old light keeper pushed his wife down the stairs, then hung himself. Now the wife haunts the property."

"I've heard that story. I don't put much credence to it though. The lunch crowd will be here shortly. You ready for another busy day?"

She smiled and adjusted her hair net. "Can't wait!" Half an hour later two other cooks arrived and the orders started coming from the waitstaff. Bruce and Heather worked fast. They were a well-oiled machine. Each knew the other's techniques and challenges, and they picked up each other's slack. When the first real break came at two in the afternoon, Heather glanced at the two auxiliary books and said, "You guys were excellent today."

Bruce liked how his sous chef always built others up. Paying compliments when he didn't think to. "Why don't you knock off for the day? Go out and have some fun. Hey - why not stop by the Spring House as see Sean?"

"I can't leave you alone."

"I'm hardly alone. I have plenty of staff here and will be able to keep up. Seriously," Bruce said. "Go on. Get outta here. Enjoy the day. Tomorrow's supposed to rain all day anyways."

Heather knew when to argue and when not to. This was one time to relent. "Alright. I'm going." Once she walked through the kitchen and out into the lobby, she took her hair net off and tossed it in the trash. Sitting in her Jeep for a moment she sent Sean a text with a happy face emoji serving as a period and headed toward the Spring House.

As she approached the Spring House, her heart quickened. Her hands were suddenly clammy, sticking to the steering wheel. For a brief moment, she thought about driving right on by.

Sean stepped out on the porch and watched Heather's Jeep navigate the long hotel driveway. He waved to her when she pulled up. She closed the door and strolled up the sloping lawn, passing the ubiquitous white Adirondack chairs lined up facing the ocean. Reaching the porch, she leaned in and gave Sean a quick embrace.

"I didn't think I'd be here so soon."

Sean smiled. "I did," he said, pulling away. "Would you like something to eat?"

"Wait a minute. What do you mean, you did? How did you know?"

He ignored her and returned inside. "Let's get some food, and then we can have the rest of the afternoon to figure out what we want to do. How does that sound?" He glanced back. "You coming?" he said, holding the door.

"Right behind you." She walked in and followed Sean to the hotel kitchen. "How did you know I would be here early?" She wouldn't let this go. Like a dog with a bone, she refused to relent.

He continued to avoid the question. Walking to the freezer, he pulled out two pieces of fish. "I hope you like salmon," he said.

Heather swept that errant strand of hair away from the corner of her mouth. "You know me better than I thought."

"It helps," Sean said as he went to the stove and grabbed a frying pan, "that Bruce knows you well. He turned the stovetop on medium and placed the two pieces of salmon in the pan. "Now, I'm not promising this will be up to Bruce's standards," he laughed, "but he has given me a few tips."

"Can I help?" Heather asked, as she watched him move effortlessly around the kitchen.

"Nope. I got this. You and Bruce aren't the only ones who know their way around a kitchen. Besides, you cook all the time. Just keep me company while I prepare our food. How long have you worked as a chef?"

"I remember cooking for my grandparents while I was in high school. One of my classes was a cooking class. In fact, speaking of my grandparents, they were how I discovered Block Island. My first visit was in the 1970s. Back when the Book Nook was at Payne's Dock."

"How did your cooking class go?"

"In order to pass I had to prepare dinner for family and friends. I made pork chops, mashed potatoes, and broccoli. My next dinner was something for the teacher and students."

Heather stepped aside as Sean grabbed a bunch of carrots from the refrigerator.

"Even before taking the cooking class," she continued, "I cooked meals at home. I've always loved cooking. I think that class cemented my desire to become a chef. When Bruce arrived on the island, I immediately befriended him by coming to the National as often as I could until he gave me a job. We've been friends ever since."

"Ambition is a good thing. Bruce is lucky to have you," Sean said, flipping the salmon.

"It may seem from the outside that there's more to our relationship because we share everything. Honestly though? There has never been any inclination on either of our parts to move our relationship in any other direction. We love working together, and that's as far as it goes. He's taught me so much and I owe him big time."

"I know what you mean. If not for him, and Tom who I've known even longer than Bruce, I'd still be a wreck. After losing Kate, the both of them rescued me."

"Hmmm." Heather said. "They're both such good people."

"Tom insisted I come to the island and offered me a place to stay. The only thing he wanted in return was occasional help managing the place. Then Bruce got in on the action." Sean explained how it all went down. "Those two were calling me every day." He drew in a breath and sighed. Checking the stove again, he pulled the pan away from the burner. "I think our fish is ready. Shall we go out to the front porch?" Sean put each slice of fish and a pile of carrots on two plates. Handing one to Heather, they grabbed a table outside, overlooking the broad Atlantic Ocean, facing east.

Several other guests were taking in the warm weather and the shade of the porch.

"Who's your new friend?" one of the nosy women asked.

Another said, "Good for you. About time you started realizing there are plenty of fish in the sea."

Now, he hid his face to keep everyone from seeing how red he'd become. He motioned to Heather and they both grabbed their plates and moved to a quiet table around the far end of the porch, toward the rear patio.

"I think we just offended those two ladies."

"And they, me. No one will bother us way over here, on the side porch."

"I love this view!" she said.

"So do I. Nothing like that green lawn sweeping down to the road and the ocean on the other side. Where else can you see so much water?"

"Amazing scene," Heather agreed.

As they ate Sean said, "Did I mention I'm considering staying on the island? Tom wants me to move here permanently. And to answer your question about how I knew you'd be here early I saw Bruce as I left this morning and asked him if he needed you after the lunch rush. I wanted him to consider letting you go a little early."

"Well, thanks for getting me some extra time off. So, you're gonna stay? That's great."

"Thinking about it. I don't have much keeping me from not staying. My brother visits sometimes from Key West. And I might have something keeping me here." He reached across the table and touched Heather's hand.

She withdrew her hand to pick up her folk and spear a bite of salmon. She tasted it. "Mmmm. Not bad." She took another bite. "I'm glad you're considering staying. I really would like to see if we have something here too."

He smiled and said, "There's definitely a connection. I feel it and think it's worth exploring. And now knowing you feel it as well makes my decision both easier and more difficult. I know Tom wants me to stay because he can use the help. And as I said before, I really have nothing keeping me in Connecticut. And I have a lot more to keep me here." He again reached across the table and rested his hand on hers. This time she did not pull her hand away.

After they finished eating, Sean gathered up their plates and utensils and they walked back to the kitchen. After rinsing off the dishes and placing them in the washer, he turned to Heather. "So, what would you like to do now?" Heather thought a minute. "Feel like going to Southeast Light. There's something there I want to see. It's been bothering me all day."

"Sounds like a plan," he said. "Let's go."

As they walked through the hotel, Tom happened by. "What's this?" he asked, seeing them. "Heather, nice to see you."

"We're headed to Southeast Light," Sean said, as they continued on their way.

"Be careful," Tom shouted. "You know that place is haunted. Today's the anniversary."

"Oh, funny," Sean said and smiled.

After Heather clicked in her seatbelt shed turned to face Sean. "Tom's right. I remember someone saying it was July when the lightkeeper pushed his wife to her death. Maybe that's why I thought the lighthouse looked different today."

Sean started the truck and headed toward Southeast Light. "It looked different?" he said. "Different how?"

Heather looked out the passenger side window. "You're gonna think I'm crazy."

He laughed. "I don't think so. Tell you what. If you tell me your story, I'll tell you mine. Then we can compare and see who's crazier." He grinned at her now.

Intrigued, Heather asked, "You've experienced something there too?"

"I'm surprised you haven't heard." They pulled into the small Southeast Light parking area just off the road by the chain link fence, and Heather looked up at the lighthouse. It was back in its proper location. Only three other vehicles were there at four-thirty. She stepped out of the vehicle and raced ahead, up the dirt driveway toward the lighthouse, leaving Sean to play catch up. Nearly running into someone, Heather looked back and saw Sean several yards behind. She stopped, waiting for him. Looking out over the property, she saw the boulder at the far end of the land, gray board fencing all around the perimeter of the property.

When Sean caught up, he said, "What's your hurry?"

"That boulder," She said. "Follow me." They traversed the wide lawn and arrived at the large boulder, which was about the size of a Volkswagen Beetle. She sat down beside the boulder. "Here," she said, tapping the dry soil. "Sit down."

"Funny," he said. "I come here sometimes when I want to be alone. In this very spot too, in fact."

Heather felt her heart flutter. It suddenly felt like they'd known each other all their lives. It felt so comfortable being in Sean's presence. She had an inclination they were a perfect match, but this was beyond all expectations. Easy and effortless were the words that came to her. She reached out to take his hand. "I didn't expect this."

He sighed. "I didn't expect it either. I want to continue seeing you. I think we're good together. I don't want to rush into anything though. Let's take this slow."

She smiled. "That's exactly how I feel. So, my story…" she said. "When I drove by here this morning on the way to work, I swore the lighthouse was back in its original position, which was right here, at this boulder. And after Tom told us that today is the anniversary, he meant that this was the day, back in the early 1900s, that the lighthouse keeper pushed his wife down the iron staircase inside the tower. So, what I saw makes sense."

At that moment, Heather felt herself pushed back against the boulder. "What the…" She attempted to stand up but immediately fell to the ground again.

Sean attempted to help her up. "Are you alright?"

A chill went through her as something brushed past her. Whatever it was made impressions in the grass as if someone were walking on it. "Do you see that?" she said, gesturing to the ground and ignoring his question. "What *is* that?" She stood up and followed the phantom footstep, which continued forming as depression in the grass, right in front of her eyes. The footsteps were leading across the wide lawn toward the lighthouse.

Then she heard a disembodied woman's voice say, *"It's not what you think."*

Another couple were walking out of the lighthouse and also saw the grass being pressed down. Heather watched as they gestured to the footsteps and then looked at each other. Heather couldn't make out what they were saying, but it was definitely an animated conversation. Drawing closer, she heard individual words. *"Ghost... murder... suicide."* But it was enough to draw a conclusion. The couple turned and raced to the parking lot at the end of the long driveway, both of them shrieking and not looking back.

Sean came to Heather's side.

"Tell me you heard that woman's voice."

His mouth agape, he couldn't believe this was happening again. "I heard it. *Kate*?" His knees felt weak. "What are you doing to me?" he said, peering up at the heavens.

The lighthouse guide stepped out then. "We'll be closing shortly," she said. "Our last tour starts now if you are interested."

Heather and Sean were the only people to address.

"Let's take the tour?" Heather asked, joining him near the lighthouse.

"Okay," he said, regaining his walking legs. He looked back at the fence located just the other side of the boulder where they had just been sitting. Just then something passed through him, and he tripped up the steps to the lighthouse porch. He righted himself and took a moment to recover his equilibrium.

"Are you okay," Heather asked.

"Yes, yes, fine. Let's go in." They stepped inside the small hallway.

The guide said, "I'm Christine." She then stepped to the door to the porch to close it, and glanced toward the boulder in the distance that marked the original position of the lighthouse when it was first erected, in 1873. Then she saw the phantom footstep impressions on the grass beside the porch steps and her pulse quickened. "What the heck? Go away, Maggie!" she said, shoeing the air. She closed the door fully and turned to face Sean and Heather.

As they walked from the hall into the room at the base of the light tower, an ethereal gust of wind coming off the water blew through the open windows of the lighthouse, slamming shut the door back to the entrance hall. Each of them attempted to open the door.

Each failed.

"It's not what you think."

This time, Christine heard it. "That--that--that's not Maggie," she said, clearly distressed. "I know Maggie's voice, having been here and heard it." As Chris continued to pull on the door knob, Christine said. "Do you know who it is?"

"Yah, it's his girlfriend, Kate." Heather said, nodding at Sean. "She passed a while ago. What we don't know is *why* she's here now, haunting Sean."

"Well, regardless… no use in attempting to get that door open. I've had to sleep in this cold tower base overnight, in that desk chair, on more than one occasion." Christine went to the adjacent table that held pamphlets about the lighthouse. A lamp stood on the table. She switched it on, bathing the room in a soft yellow light. "Something has Maggie disturbed. I've never found her to be violent, though. She's just a sad soul who's trapped here."

"That's not what I've heard," Heather said. "I've heard that Maggie likes to lock people into rooms and closets. Like we are right now. Men especially… they get the worst treatment. I've heard she sometimes moves furniture around in the dead of night, and one young man tripped over a bookshelf that Maggie placed at the top of those stairs. He fell to his death."

A low moaning began that seemed to start at the top of the lighthouse and work its way to the bottom. The sound wave pulsed through the three of them, almost becoming a physical presence. The light on the pamphlet table flickered off and on, then finally off. The group waited. And waited. Silent. The light didn't turn back on.

Christine smiled at Heather in the dim room. "You're right about Maggie being particularly difficult toward men. But you have to understand her good reason. After all, a man did push her down those stairs to hear death." Christine pointed at the start of the long spiral staircase behind her.

The moaning started again. Now it almost sounded as if a word were forming. *"Nooooooo."*

"Did you hear that?" Heather asked.

"Kate?" Sean asked, staring into the air as he walked to the edge of the staircase. "Ka...Ka...Kate?" His voice shook. And now he trembled for a completely different reason. Out of the corner of his eye, he saw something white slowly begin descending the staircase from above. He glanced back at Christine and Heather. "Are you seeing this?" He quickly turned back to looked, in awe, and the figure on the staircase. A moment later the apparition vanished.

Christine stepped toward Sean. "You're Sean Wolf!" "My God, I should have known. I thought you looked familiar. When you said Kate was your girlfriend, that's when I realized I had heard that name before. But I don't understand what Kate has to do with Mad Maggie."

Heather swept that same problem strand of hair away from her eyes again. "Is that what you were going to tell me, Sean? That it was you who brought the Palatine back for everyone to see?"

"Not just me," Sean said. "Kate's the one who did that. But yes. It happened to be my grief for her that brought the ship here."

"So, why do you think she's back?" Christine asked.

"Well," he said, taking another look up the stairs. "I have a theory. I'm still working it out, so bear with me. What does she the voice keep saying?"

Heather and Christine glanced at each other and simultaneously said, "It's not what you think."

Sean smiled. "Correct. So, what's *not* what we think it is? What has every islander been told about the haunting here at Southeast Light? Why does Mad Maggie remain here? Why does any spirit stay and not move on?" He waited for an answer. "C'mon. This isn't difficult."

The lighthouse suddenly shook. The entire building rocked off its foundation. Tables and chairs fell to the ground. Pictures dropped to the floor, their framed glass shattering into pieces. The door shook so violently, it seemed as if it would break away from its jamb. The sky outside the small windows went completely dark, and so too the room at the base of the light tower they were trapped in. That same low moaning sound started again.

Heather went to Sean and wrapped her arms around him for comfort. "What's happening?" she asked.

Sean felt her shaking against his chest. He pushed her to arm's length and looked deeply into her eyes. "It's alright," he said. "I know what this is." As he turned back to the stairs, he saw into the past for the first time.

Sean's eyes were open but he couldn't see what was happening in current time. It was as if he was watching a movie but in real life. On a hot July night, Maggie was awakened by a distress call out on the ocean. She reached over to wake her husband. "Mike. Mike. Wake up. There's a boat out there. It needs help. Quick. Let's get dressed."

Mike rolled over in bed, pulling the covers up to his chest. Finally, after another shove from his wife, he roused himself. He made his way to the stairs, and in the dim light he didn't see or expect to see Maggie. He felt himself brush past something, and then heard a loud scream but it wasn't until he heard a thud at the bottom of the staircase that he realized what had happened. There was Maggie, lying in a clump, blood spilling out from her face and head.

He raced to where she lay. "Oh no!" he cried out, taking the love of his life in his arms. "Noooooooo! Noooooooo!"

Holding Maggie's lifeless body, he knew his own life was now over too. No one would believe this was an accident. He had no close friends here after coming to the island only this past year. He couldn't go on. Not without his Maggie. The townspeople would convict him, and truth be told, he'd probably convict himself as well. The couple were constantly at odds with each other when in public, but it wasn't like that in private. He walked stoically to the basement where there was an old meat hook hanging from the ceiling. He stared at it for a long while, gathering the strength to do what he knew he must. He couldn't live without his Maggie, and he couldn't live knowing he'd be tried and convicted before being provided the opportunity to defend himself. With tears streaming down his face, he meticulously unbuckled his belt, swung it over the hook, and strapped the other end around his neck.

Images passed through his mind before he let go. Cooking dinner for each other and helping clean up after. Strolling the beach, holding hands. Kissing under the starlight as it played off the water.

Seeing these scenes, Sean realized that this was not an unhappy marriage. And Maggie's death was not murder. It had been an accident.

"It's not what you think," the voice said again, louder this time.

Tears streamed down Christine's face after she too heard the disembodied voice, which she instantly recognized as Mad Maggie's—from other times Maggie had said things when Christine was alone in the lighthouse. After Sean told Heather and Christine what he had just witnessed in his time-travel trance, Christine believed every word and said, "We condemned a man without knowing the full story. And we condemned Maggie to this purgatory because she only wanted closure."

Just then the lighthouse exploded into a white light—and Kate stepped out of the light—and the past and the present converged. She saw Maggie, in the past, lying in a lump at the bottom of the light tower stairs. She reached out to her, touching her wounds.

Maggie stirred and raised her head. Bringing her hands up, she felt for the blood. There was none. "What? What? Who—who are you?"

"I'm the conduit." Kate pulled Maggie up off the floor. "We have one more soul to save tonight." She walked down the same steps that Mike took that fateful night, Maggie trailing close behind.

"Nooooooo!" A terrifying scream let loose from Maggie when she saw Mike's lifeless body swaying in the shadows of the basement. When Kate touched Mike's neck, he shuddered. His eyes opened. For the first time in over a hundred years, he saw his wife.

Sean lifted him up off the wicked meat hook and Mike raced over to her. Embracing her, he pulled back. "How... how?" He couldn't muster any other words. He turned to the other woman in the room. "Did you do this?"

Ignoring the question, Kate said, "It's time to go." And she led them out of the basement, passing the three people in the lighthouse: Sean, Heather, and Christine.

Kate glanced at Sean and Heather. "Follow us," she said before continuing up spiral staircase with Maggie and Mike, to the top of the lighthouse, where the Fresnel lens sat in the lantern room. Once in the lantern room, Kate let out a frosty breath. The room clouded over in the cool mist of her exhalation. "I'm so happy you found each other. The four of you." She smiled at the two couples. "Take care of Sean, Heather." Then to Sean, she said, "See? Didn't I tell you you'd find someone again?"

He reached out to her, but his hands went straight through her.

Kate turned to Maggie and Mike and smiled. "Are you ready?"

They nodded and then the three of them floated into the light coming from inside the Fresnel lens, becoming one with the lighthouse, and the room flared with an intense white light.

Kate's voice hung in the air. "I'll always love you, Sean. But now you have someone else who loves you too."

When Sean and Heather arrived back at the Spring House, they were both so exhausted and feeling like they were in a dream, they tripped up the foyer door threshold together and fell through the main entrance, knocking the flower table beside the door over, making a hell of a racket. Tom emerged from his bedroom at the top of the main staircase. "What's all the racquet down there? My guests are trying to sleep, not to mention me."

He looked down and saw Sean and Heather picking themselves up off the floor. He dashed down to their sides. "Oh my God, are you guys all right?"

"We just lost our balance is all."

Heather nodded.

"Are you two drunk?" Tom sniffed the air near them.

"Not on your life."

"Are you sure you're alright? You two look like you've seen a ghost."

"Oh, more than one," Heather said.

"Huh?" was all that Tom could utter.

Sean smiled, put his right arm around Heather and patted Tom on the shoulder with his left hand. "Night, old friend," he said, and left Tom standing there at the bottom of the staircase looking somewhat perplexed.

Sean and Heather made their way slowly to Sean's room, and closed the door.

Night Swimming

Amanda Dodge loved North Light. It was seven-thirty when she arrived at golden hour, that hour before sunset. The wind was strong that day, so she decided to park as close as she could to the pond, in the lot directly in front of Sachem Pond. She grabbed her Canon DSLR and her tripod from the trunk, and walked to the beach at the edge of the parking lot. Once on the beach she had to stop every few minutes to catch her breath, for the wind was whipping hard 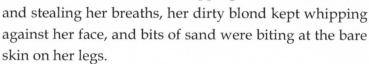 and stealing her breaths, her dirty blond kept whipping against her face, and bits of sand were biting at the bare skin on her legs.

Over the years, Amanda had developed asthma and she often felt short of breath. She frequently found herself stopping to rest before moving on and reluctantly always carried her rescue inhaler. She had numerous chronic issues that gave her pause, and at times she wondered whether she could continue doing everything she loved. Photography helped keep her busy enough to keep that thought at bay. Most of the time. People raved about the photographs her lens captured on Block Island, including the most famous and accomplished Block Island photographer of them all, Mr. Malcolm Greenaway. In fact, Amanda carried his 600mm lens on her camera. Malcolm rarely spent time at his studio, but Amanda knew that Malcom showed up every Wednesday morning just to collect his mail. When she appeared at his shop, her visit wasn't to discuss photography, per se. Her objective in meeting Malcolm was to gain a new client.

Partnering with a photographer who also ran the type of business she did would definitely boost her business on the island. When Amanda realized that, she gathered her courage and decided if the timing was right, she would approach him. Sticking out her hand, she said, "Hi, Mr. Greenaway. I'm Amanda Dodge. I have a social —."

"I know who you are," he said, stopping her. "I've been following your work for some time now. You've got quite the eye, Ms. Dodge."

She turned away, masking her blush. "Well. Th... th... thank you," she stammered, clearly embarrassed by the compliment.

Malcolm walked farther into his studio, beckoning Amanda to follow. He showed her to a side room. Here, a desk and two leather chairs were positioned by a window. "Have a seat," he said, motioning to one of the chairs as he took a seat behind the desk. "As I said, I've been following your work. I'm intrigued by how you capture the sunset. Your use of water against the sand and scrub brings out their colors beautifully. I especially like the different perspectives you get of the North Light. You know what you're doing. That's for sure."

Amanda couldn't believe this. Here was a professional giving her wave upon wave of compliments. "I don't know what to say," she said, blushing and turning away. Malcolm's photos hung throughout the studio, but one in his office really caught her eye. It was a wide angle shot of the Southeast Light, taken from the top of the Mohegan Bluffs, with the sun rising, which created a red and orange color throughout the sky and ground. She walked over to inspect the picture. "Talk about perspective. Now that's an amazing shot. The sunrise is gorgeous. And just look at the ocean. It must have been frigid that morning. You can almost feel the icy mist coming off the water."

At that moment, Malcolm was hooked. "You're the first person to recognize that the picture was taken in the middle of winter," he said. "I'm impressed."

Over the next year, they began shooting together and sharing their work with each other. And slowly, over the course of their friendship, Amanda was able to secure him as another client. Once Malcolm noticed her,

her success grew. He invited her to showcase some of her best photos in his downtown studio. And they became inseparable.

Before meeting Malcolm, Amanda ran a pretty successful business on her own. She had made her living as a social media consultant and web host, managing her client's websites and social media presence. Since she worked from her computer, she was able to amass a loyal clientele in Connecticut as well. She'd gone to The Chamber of Commerce on Block Island several times, and her dedication to networking paid for her success. One client, who she had signed just a few months ago, was Michelle Joy. She ran a past life regression business called Into the Past. Her storefront was located down the street from the National Hotel, but being halfway down Chapel Street made it a bit out of the way. Plus, being an esoteric business made promoting it a challenge. But Amanda never backed down. She met with Michelle several times since their initial meeting at a chamber event, where they learned as much as possible about each other's businesses and strategized on how they could help one another. They agreed to work together on a contingency, month-to-month, for six-months, then reevaluate. As they approached the six-month mark, Amanda's marketing had succeeded in earning more business for Michelle. In fact, Into the Past had brought in more business than it had in the past eighteen-months following Amanda's help. Through email campaigns, a new user-friendly website, and some good old-fashioned word-of-mouth, Michelle's business not only boomed, it blossomed beyond both their expectations. This is why Amanda found herself in such high demand. She brought results where no one else could.

Things were going great for her, business wise. With Amanda constantly being out with her camera, she developed a positive reputation. She'd had a meeting with a prospective client a week earlier who lived in Connecticut. They were going to firm up details within the week before he left.

People were drawn to her and it was easy to see why. She loved talking about photography with anyone who'd listen. In fact, she loved talking business with anyone who would listen. People wouldn't believe she was a true introvert at heart because you couldn't get her to stop talking about what she loved. But contrary to popular belief, that is one of the more prominent attributes of introverts. If you get them talking about their passion, you'll wish they'd stop.

❖ ❖ ❖

One day, after setting up her camera with the 600mm lens on the tripod at the parking lot between the ocean and Sachem Pond, she started taking pictures of North Light in the distance. As she snapped the shutter button, she heard a splash. It didn't sound like a bird or fish. It sounded like someone diving into the water. She looked out at the ocean. "Funny," she said out loud. "I didn't see anyone out here when I arrived." She chose to ignore the splashing and refocus on her task at hand — getting the best possible pictures at sunset of the North Light.

More splashing about. This time the sound came from behind her. It sounded like the splashing was coming from the pond.

Who on earth would be swimming in that muck? she questioned.

She squinted in the dusk and tried her best to see who it was, but to no avail. Next, she swung her tripod around hoping she could zoom in on whoever it may be. All she could make out was a head bobbing in the murky water at least a third of the way across the pond. Great, not only do I have asthma and a bum leg, but now I'm seeing a creature out in the pond. Have I lost it?

The sun disappeared over the horizon of the North Point dunes, leaving everything bathed in darkness. Amanda took a few more shots, this time moving her tripod up the beach to get a different angle. With each step taken, she found herself breathing more heavily. She stopped twice to catch her breath before carrying the heavy camera setup to another point some two hundred feet from her last position.

She again wondered whether all this work that sapped her energy was truly worth the effort. She shook off the thought and moved father up the beach, closer to the lighthouse. She took a few more shots using the rising moon for both light and a backdrop, then scrolled through what she captured. Pleased with the shots, she packed up, then walked back to her Mini Cooper. The wind picked up more, beating against her, blowing her hair all around.

There were times when she had come to the decision to pack everything in and move forward in her life and go on to a different creative path. Concentrate more on her social media business perhaps? Before she met Malcolm, Amanda had all but decided to give up photography, but Heather had talked her out of it.

Amanda sat in her Mini and stared into the dark pond beyond the hood.

Photography turned out to be a blessing and a curse. A blessing because it took her mind off the phobia she experienced about others seeing her disability. And a curse because of the pain and exhaustion she felt after taking her pictures and returning to her vehicle. The latter was why she took time to recover by sitting in her car, her head resting against the headrest, and letting out a long sigh. She closed her eyes and thought of how Malcom never minded. How relaxed she felt with him. Although, that wouldn't make matters any easier for her health.

Once the pain in her leg subsided, she headed home. Even at this hour, on Corn Neck Road to town, cars continued to move about, some at a faster speed than necessary. Tourists didn't have the same knowledge as islanders on the nuances of the road, so at least three or four times during the height of summer, especially on this road in the dark of night, there happened to be a fender bender. Fortunately, there were seldom any damages other than a bruised ego from the person who caused the accident.

She turned onto Dodge Street and smiled when she saw the street sign. It was named after her family. Her great grandfather, Tristram Dodge, helped fund a school on the island and served at first selectman for fifteen years. For that contribution to the town, the Board of Selectmen voted to rename a local road after him. The townspeople all cheered when the first Dodge Street sign went up. Fifteen years ago, in the wake of a town beautification project, she had convinced the town to let her have the old street sign. Amanda secured the Dodge Street sign that now hung proudly in her living room.

As she turned onto Water Street, passing the National Hotel, she thought about Bruce's excellent mahi mahi and how she was meeting Heather for lunch there tomorrow. Of all the entries on the menu, the mahi mahi was her favorite. Her thoughts then turned directly to Bruce. Maybe he would show up. If only she could tell him how she felt. If only she didn't feel so self-conscious about all her physical challenges. If only.

She turned onto Spring Street and thought about her friend, Ester Lindstrom. They only lived a few miles apart. There were only a lucky few that Ester cherished. Amanda was one of them. They typically met at Ester's for morning coffee at least once a week. Amanda would have to call in a couple of days. Ester was an almost seventy-year-old Block Islander who had lived on Block Island since the late 1950s. Not a true islander, because to be considered an islander, you had to be born here. However, Ester became accepted as an islander when folks spoke with her and learned that she had grown up much the same they had, in a small fishing community on the other side of the world in Sweden.

About a mile past Ester's property, Amanda turned down a dirt road. She smiled as her house came into view. She grabbed her camera and lens, walked in, and placed it on her drafting table. Tomorrow, she thought, eyeing the camera. Time for bed now.

❖ ❖ ❖

"Hey! How's my BFF doing?" Amanda asked Heather as she stood up and they embraced.

"Great day for lunch at the National, don't ya think?"

They sat on the porch as usual. The entire porch was filled with tourists. The cacophony of several conversations going on at once made it almost impossible to hear one another. Right across from the ferry docks, people could keep a watchful eye on their ferry as they enjoyed a meal or drink before departing for the mainland. Even at one o'clock in the afternoon, the restaurant was at near capacity.

A waitress came by with two glasses of water and recognized Heather. With a smile, she said, "Well, well. Fancy seeing you here on your day off. I'll be back in a few to take your order."

A warm breeze blew through the porch, scattering several napkins to the ground. There was often a soft breeze on this island, no matter what the season. The sun blazed in the sky and not a cloud could be seen, but that warm breeze helped to keep the humidity at bay. Any movement in the air helped. Amanda didn't do well in humidity, so she felt grateful for the breeze.

At the table next to them, a couple were in a heated discussion. The people around them couldn't help but overhear. Amanda tried to ignore it and concentrate on talking to Heather, but the volume of the couple's voices kept intruding.

"Don't you see, Ed?!" the woman said. "It's all that damn swimming you're doing at night. You come home stinking to High Heaven from Sachem Pond and then disappear into the shower for a half-hour or more. I'd almost think you were having an affair. I don't even know why you swim there when we have the entire ocean for a backyard."

Amanda froze as she overheard this. It was Ed Ball swimming at Sachem Pond? Why on earth? She'd recognized Ed and Cheryl from various chamber events, but she couldn't recall the business they were in.

I can understand why she's freaking out. That pond must be full of bacteria and leeches.

"Amanda? Earth to Amanda," Heather said, snapping Amanda out of her thoughts.

"I'm sorry. I zoned out for a moment. She raised her voice a bit so Heather to hear her.

"What is it you wanted to talk about?"

"Well," Amanda took in a breath and let it out. "I know I've said this before, but I'm thinking of giving up photography and island life. It's killing me to even consider it, Heather. At the same time, it's killing me to continue on here. And my asthma isn't making it any easier. I know every doctor I go to tells me that walking is the best thing I can do, but I simply don't know how much longer I can continue doing that. I get winded so easily." She shuddered. Amanda felt close to breaking down.

Heather reached across the table. Taking Amanda's hand in her own, she said, "I certainly can't walk in your shoes. But I understand the pain you're having because I've seen it and I've watched you struggle." She withdrew her hand and grabbed her glass for water for a sip. She then smiled at her friend. "But I've also seen the joy on your face when you get ready to go out with your camera. I've seen how excited you get about finding the perfect shot and how much time and care you take editing your photography." Heather brushed her hand through her hair and looked directly into Amanda's eyes. "I certainly can't tell you what to do,

Amanda. Only you know that. And whether you see it or not, I also know how much it bothers you that you're not as mobile as you wish. Honestly, I think your photography helps you more than you know."

The couple at the next table were still in the midst of arguing when the woman stood up and pushed her chair aside. "I'm not sure how much longer I can do this, Ed. We've been having this same discussion for months now, and you're not willing to compromise." With that she walked away.

This left Ed at the table by himself. He quickly grabbed his wallet and threw a few bills down, then stood up. Amanda noted that he was clearly in some pain, not from his wife yelling and walking out, but some kind of physical pain. He grimaced and winced as he made his way down the front staircase to the sidewalk below, grunting loudly.

Ed was clearly flustered as he reached the bottom of the stairs. He looked around, darting his eyes back and forth. "I'm so sorry," he said to one in particular. Ed stood there for a moment, and leaned against the railing. He stretched until he heard a satisfying crack. He then smiled slightly and ambled away to look for his wife.

After that, the deck seemed like a church in the middle of service; quiet and peaceful.

"I'm not sure what to do if I give up photography. Maybe I'll—"

Amanda stopped mid-sentence when head chef, Bruce Pigott strolled over. She shrunk back into her chair and covered her face, clearly embarrassed to see him.

"Hi, girls," Bruce said, standing between them. "Amanda. Hope you're doing well."

"Mm-mm." She smiled and glanced up at him. Then she turned away again, her face flushed. Turning back, she said, "Thanks for asking." Stretching her legs, she winced a bit. "Just this damn leg keeps me from doing all I want. It's what Heather and I have been discussing."

"Bruce moved to an empty chair at the table. "May I?"

They both nodded and he sat.

"Look. We all have problems and we all have ways to get our mind off them," he said. "Mine's cooking. If I could no longer cook, well... you wouldn't want to be around me." He chuckled. "Ain't that right, Heather? And you? Your talent is photography. "

Amanda looked at Bruce. Her face continued to flush, and an electricity coursed through her body. She smiled again and shifted her legs under the table. All this attention felt nice, but she didn't feel like it was warranted this time. She knew her photography shined. She'd been told so by everyone who knew her, but having Bruce say so felt especially gratifying. "Well, thank you," she said.

Nodding, he surveyed the table. "Guess I'll let you girls finish up. Good to see you again, Amanda." With that, Bruce left the table and went inside.

Amanda smiled as she watched him leave. Realizing her friend saw this, she quickly covered for herself, attempting to sidetrack Heather. "That was nice that he stopped by," Amanda said, not sure if that was distracting enough. At this point, though, she didn't really care anymore. She'd have to deal with it.

"What was that?" Heather whispered after Bruce left, staring straight through Amanda as if she could see into her very soul. "Do you like him or something?"

"What? No."

"C'mon, Amanda. How long have we known each other? You're blushing."

Knowing she'd been caught, Amanda relented. "Alright." She drew in a breath. "So, I like him."

"Don't you think he should know?"

"Yeah, but look at me." Amanda felt on the verge of breaking down again. She sucked in a breath. "My breathing is a challenge and getting worse. The last thing I want is to become a burden on someone else. Besides, I like my independence. I like that I can go home, and no one ever telling me it's time to eat or go to bed or when to get up. If anyone knows me, it's you. You understand how much space I need. By living alone, I can do what I want when I want."

"That's all well and good but we all need a support system, especially living on the island. And what if

Bruce feels the same way? Don't you think he should have the opportunity to see if there's a connection with you? How will he know that you're interested if you don't speak up?" Amanda nodded. "I can lay the groundwork but before I agree to do anything, I have to have your word that you won't hurt him. You remember what happened with Grace? How devastated he felt when he discovered her..." Heather paused here. "And I didn't even know Grace. You and Bruce are my best friends. I would love nothing more than to see you two hit it off. And, you'd better have me as your maid-of-honor!" Heather smiled before laughing out loud.

Amanda shook her head. "C'mon, we haven't even had a first date, and you're already planning our wedding? I can assume you'll help me with Bruce now?"

Heather agreed and said she'd talk to Bruce the next day.

❖ ❖ ❖

Like clockwork, Amanda woke at six-thirty. She dragged herself out of bed and jumped in the shower. After getting dressed she headed to the kitchen for coffee. This was her favorite part of the day — sitting at the kitchen table, drinking her coffee, and looking out at the water. It's why she could never think about leaving Block Island and living anywhere else. Although she understood that at some point her health challenges could change that. In the future she would have to be closer to a hospital or a medical care center, two things the island couldn't provide. But the future wasn't today.

Heather was right in one respect. There would come a time when Amanda needed someone close by. Maybe — she shuddered at the thought — even having someone live with her. Amanda had lived on her own for nearly twenty years. She bought her house on Spring Street when she turned twenty-five. She didn't know how she'd adjust to having another person living with her, but that eventuality didn't need to be determined today. She took one more look at the water outside her kitchen window and sighed. "I love it here!" she said out loud.

She prepared her regular breakfast: an egg white omelet with mushrooms, tomatoes, and mozzarella. While her eggs began to simmer, she reached for her phone and texted Heather. *Hope you have an amazing day. And thank you for all you do for me.*

She ate her breakfast at the drafting table where she kept her MacBook. She opened it up and began to review each image from her photo shoot last night. After opting to keep the best fifteen images, she deleted the rest and started the editing process. An hour later, the finished photos were uploaded to her website, and she emailed a link of the new content to Malcolm.

Her thoughts drifted to Ed Ball — and the ruckus his wife had made at on the National porch — and his nightly swims at Sachem Pond. Determined to discover what made Sachem Pond so special to him, she made the decision to return that night.

Heather also fluttered back into her thoughts. Amanda remembered her saying how much joy she saw Amanda have while editing her pictures and being out and about with her camera. Heather was right and Bruce was right. Photography was her passion. How could she give that up?

Thinking about Bruce again, she realized she did need to talk to him. At nine-fifteen, she grabbed her camera, purse and keys, and double checked to make sure she had her reading material: Jonathan Carroll's *Bathing the Lion*. Taking one last look around, Amanda walked out the front door.

She sat in her vehicle for a moment, considering the consequences of her actions. Would Bruce feel the same way? If he didn't, would he let her down easily? One thing Amanda knew, she could no longer see him and not get flustered. If Heather noticed, it certainly wouldn't be long until Bruce realized something as well. She headed out, passing the Spring House, and knew she had to stop in and talk with Tom Norris. He'd been looking for a new web host, and word trickled down that he wanted to talk to Amanda.

When she pulled into town, Amanda passed several handicap parking signs. Several of her friends, including Heather, had implored her to apply for a permit. Amanda always declined. "The moment I need a handicap sticker is the moment I give up," she said.

"Besides, the more I walk, the stronger I'll get." Her heart began to pound as she looked up at the National Hotel. Her future began somewhere inside; whether it would be a future with Bruce or without she wouldn't know until she confronted her trepidation. She found a parking spot in the public lot near the Old Harbor Landing. She knew from Heather that he took a beach break between ten and eleven. Amanda pulled her phone out. Ten-fifteen. It was all, or nothing at all.

She looked toward the beach to the left of the Old Harbor parking lot. Bruce was sitting in a folding chair at the water's edge. She felt a little sick to her stomach but she went back to her vehicle and grabbed her own beach chair and purse. Then she walked down the path to where Bruce was sitting.

"You stalking me?" he asked when he looked up and saw her approach.

She stared at him for a moment with her mouth agape, not sure what to say. Taking a breath and letting it out, she finally found her voice. "Actually, yes," she said, placing her chair beside his. Looking around, she felt happy there were only a few other people on this small beach, giving them a bit more privacy. It was actually a bit surprising there were so few people, considering the time of day and season.

"Um... I do... actually want to talk to you." She adjusted herself in her chair so that she faced him. "Um," she said again. "I'm... I'm wondering if you...

if... if you'd like... if you'd like to go out sometime?" There. She'd said it. The question was out.

"I actually would like that," he said. Smiling back at her, he paused and looked down at his feet in the sand. The cool water touched their toes as a wave washed onto the shore and ran up the beach. "I kinda felt there may be some chemistry between us, especially the other afternoon when you and Heather were having lunch. I saw you look away." He drew in a breath. "I didn't understand why until later that evening when Heather started feeding me some line about you. That's when I realized perhaps you felt the same way. Am I right?"

Amanda sighed. She nodded. "You're right."

"I'm glad Heather spoke to me." He looked around the beach. "I love it here. Kinda quiet and small. It's where I like to go when I want to be alone." He grew quiet then and closed his eyes, taking in the calm the ocean produced. He then turned to look at her. Reaching across the two chairs, he took Amanda's hand and squeezed it. "I really am happy that Heather said something." He moved his feet through the water again as it ambled across the sand after the flash of a wave.

"This is so nice," Amanda said. "I can see why you like this spot."

"Yes. So peaceful," he said. Bruce closed his eyes and took in the salty Block Island air. "I could sit here forever, but unfortunately for us, work calls." He took out his phone and checked the time. "I should be getting back. Let's talk later." They exchanged numbers.

Amanda smiled to herself, watching Bruce as he headed up the incline by the breakwater and crossed the street back to the National.

"Well," she said, out loud. "That worked out better than I anticipated." She grabbed Jonathan Carroll's book out of her purse. She had met Mr. Carroll once at a writers' conference in Rhode Island. That was almost thirty years ago. Mr. Carroll was the master of ceremonies the first year she attended. She hadn't started reading his books at the time. Looking back, she wished she had. The way he constructed a sentence was pure magic. She finally discovered his works several years ago and read his entire older collection. There was one more to read after this one, then what? It's why she made sure to read each book slowly. While she could have read his work every day, she also never wanted to reach the end of any of his books.

The beach started to collect a few locals and some walkers, most of whom recognized Amanda. They nodded and let her return to her book.

Heaven, she thought, letting out a breath. There was nowhere else she'd rather be. As she read for a couple of hours, the little beach ebbed and flowed as people came and went. Occasionally she put her book down to make casual conversation with passersby. It's one of the ways she sometimes found new clients.

Never afraid to talk to people, she constantly found herself the center of attention. The only time she felt intimidated happened to be when she was in the mix of dozens of people. That's when the introvert hangover happened and she found herself retreating to her safe place: also known as her home office. Glancing at her phone, it read a little before two. Good, Amanda thought. Just enough time to grab a quick bite to eat. "Finn's, here I come."

She locked her belongings in her car, then walked over to Finn's Seafood.

She strolled over to the order window, then changed her mind about dining in. She'd order takeout instead and bring it to Sachem Pond. Maybe a stroll around the pond might yield some clues as to why Ed swims there.

"Hey Amanda. How are you?" Gary peered through the order window.

"Why, if it's not *thee* Gary Mott. How've you been? It must be what, two days since I last saw you?" she said with a laugh.

"Sounds about right. I'm doing ok. What can I get you?"

She knew he liked her. They had gone on a couple of dates but she never felt a connection. Gary felt okay with it, and they stayed friends.

"How 'bout crab cakes and a bowl of clam chowder?"

"You got it." Fifteen minutes later, Gary walked out to the deck and handed her her order. "Heading out on a photo jaunt?"

"Uhhh… yeah," she said, placing the box on a gray-painted picnic table. She reached into her pocket and took her phone out. "What do I owe?" She opened her Apple Wallet and clicked her debit card.

"Twenty-five even." Gary scanned her phone. "Good luck tonight."

"Thanks, Gary. We'll talk again soon."

Amanda felt a bit guilty about telling a half truth, but she hadn't mentioned anything to anyone about spotting Ed at the pond. She certainly wasn't about to share her real reason with Gary.

She arrived at Sachem Pond at two-thirty. Her leg was acting up a bit so she ate in the car, then tilted the seat back to rest.

She awoke at five and was surprised at how long she had napped for. I hope I didn't miss him, she thought. Like last night, no other vehicles were in the parking lot. "Hopefully this will pay off," she said aloud, and then deicide to read a bit more while she waited. She grabbed her folding chair and sat down next to her car. Just as she found the page where she had left off, she heard a splash. "You've got to be kidding me!" she said out loud. "Ed!"

She put everything back in her vehicle, tucked her phone into her purse, and walked to the spot closest to where she heard the splash. Amanda followed the swimmer with her eyes

"Ed," she shouted. He arose from the murk and headed to shore. When she finally reached him, her body was in such a way that she bent forward to grabbed her knees. Taking several deep breaths, she managed to gather herself a bit. She reached in her pocket and took out her rescue inhaler. After two puffs, she felt stronger. "This stupid breathing is not making me happy," she said.

Ed turned to her. He looked surprised, and his legs wouldn't move, almost as if he were trapped in quicksand. He looked back at the water before turning to Amanda. Not knowing which way to go, he opted to stay where his feet were planted.

"It was you here last night, Ed? Amanda said, when she faced him.

Ed was covered head to toe in a layer of pond scum. He took a towel and wiped the gunk off. The smell was so strong her eyes watered. "Why swim in Sachem Pond when the clean ocean is right over there?"

He drew in a breath. "I know, I stink. It's the pond." He wiped his arms. "A small price to pay for the benefits."

Amanda wrinkled her nose. "A small price to pay for what benefits?"

Ed realized he had two options. He could speak the truth or fabricate a lie. He thought Amanda looked like she could use the help herself. But if he let her in on his secret, he hoped she would remain silent about it. But he didn't want to give up his alone-time here at the pond, or to divulge his discovery.

"What benefits?" Amanda tried again. "Are you talking about the fight you had with your wife when I saw you at the National?"

Here was his out. Ed could say yes, and she'd be none the wiser. He could keep the real reason for swimming here to himself, and the secret would stay submerged. Watching her struggle with breathing, however, gave him pause. This was why a part of him wanted to tell her the truth. Deep in his heart, Ed Ball was a good man and he didn't like to see others suffer. Still, he didn't really know Amanda, or if he could trust her, so he felt some trepidation. What if she told others? What if when others discovered the secret all the magic disappeared? He continued to weigh his options when Amanda cleared her throat and took one more deep breath.

Reaching for her inhaler again, she puffed once. The rush from the albuterol helped—but not enough. She coughed more, attempting to clear whatever was in her throat. She took several deep breaths, but that didn't work either. No matter what she tried, her breathing became shallower. And the more she tried to catch her breath, the more difficult breathing became. Huffing and puffing, she bent down to her knees again and took a breath. Bending down, however, made it only more difficult to breathe. She tried breathing in through her nose and out through her mouth, another exercise she learned. Nothing worked. Now Amanda began to panic. She hadn't had an attack like this since last November. And everything she thought she knew, everything she was taught to do during an attack, failed her.

Ed made the decision at that moment as he watched her struggle. "Alright," he said, looking out at Sachem Pond. "You have to trust me." She could do nothing but nod. Even that gesture was an immense struggle.

Ed reached down and picked her up. "The pond," he said, "helps alleviate my back pain. But the effect only happens in the evening, an hour before sunset and an hour after. And for some odd reason only during July and August."

Amanda stared at him, not sure what to say or if she could say anything.

"I have my suspicions that the warm water and longer daylight has something to do with it," he continued. "I've been swimming here every evening, and my back feels better now than it ever has. I don't know if it will have the same effect on your breathing, but we can try."

She looked at him apprehensively and did a quick glance around the pond.

"I promise it's safe."

Amanda nodded. When they reached the pond's edge, he stopped and he looked at her. "Before I go in with you, I have to tell you something. My grandfather told me about this pond, but he couldn't figure out why the effect only worked two months out of the year. One thing he said, though, is that if you swim in the pond, it will take something from you just as it gives you something." Ed eyed Amanda again. "My grandfather used to say, 'All magic comes with a price.' The good thing is I haven't had anything taken from me... yet."

With what little energy Amanda had left, she raised her hand and pointed to the pond. Nodding, she took one more shallow breath and said, "Go."

Ed walked into the pond, carrying Amanda, and once waist deep he placed Amanda's entire body in the water. When she felt the water envelope her, a spark of energy went through her body. She gasped out, almost as if taking her first breath. She looked at herself and saw sparks rising off her skin. She glowed as the sun set and the night hours became darker. Gasping out again, she couldn't find her voice. She simply turned to Ed and tilted her head to the side, questioning him as best she could. She hoped he'd understand the gesture. Continuing to take shallow breaths so as not to overtax her lungs, she attempted one deep breath in. To her dismay, it dizzied her a little, but she had expected that. The last time she experienced an attack so severe, the same thing had happened. That one deep breath exasperated the medicine she'd been given. She needed that breath. As she settled down, Amanda continued to feel energy coursing through her legs, through her arms, through her hands—on any place her body touched water, and into her lungs. Amanda let go of Ed. "What is that?" she finally asked.

"I told you," Ed said. "There's magic here. Block Island is full of magic. Some places are more magical than others. Sachem Pond has been blessed with healing attributes."

Amanda gasped in again and let out one long breath. Feeling better with each breath, she said, "I don't understand. How come no one knows about this?"

Ed shifted his feet under the water and stared back to shore. Almost as if asking his grandfather for answers, he looked up at the sky. Before he could come up with a feasible answer, he noticed the disappearing shoreline. The time to return was drawing near. "C'mon," he said. "We should head in now."

They both turned and pushed their way through the water. When they reached the shore, Ed said, "This used to be an open secret. Everyone who knew about it has long since passed on or left the island. As far as I know, my grandfather was the last to know about the pond's magic. When he passed, the secret became mine. And now, it's yours." Ed bore his eyes into Amanda, hoping she understood. Just in case, he said, "You can't tell anyone."

She agreed. "Okay."

When they stepped out of the water, Amanda saw the specks of water on her arms and legs glow momentarily, before fading out and leaving only the water behind. She took in a breath, still not quite sure how she survived. "Wait a minute," she said, glancing at Ed. "Didn't you say that the pond expects something in return? What does it take?"

"One thing I can tell you is that it hasn't taken anything from me."

Amanda laughed out loud. "Are you serious?"

"What do you mean?" Ed asked, raising his brow. Looking back at the pond, he said, "It hasn't."

"Then what was that argument you had with your wife? Don't you see? That's what the pond took from you — your relationship with your wife."

He took a step back and stumbled over a stone. "I never saw that." He felt the tears come then. "Oh, my God! What have I done?" Tears continued to stream down his face, and he collapsed to the ground. Hugging his knees, he looked up at Amanda. "How could I not have seen that? What am I gonna do?"

"You're going to tell her the truth," Amanda said. "I've learned that keeping things to yourself doesn't help you or anyone else." She thought about Bruce and realized this to be truer now than ever now. Maybe they could have a future if she could breathe easier. It was then that she thought about what the pond might take from her, and she suddenly understood the ramifications of swimming there. What if, like Ed, the pond took away the budding relationship with Bruce? It was something she did not want to think about.

"Would you like a ride back, Ed?" she asked, breaking her thoughts. "It's dark now. And you said it yourself, you're out later than usual."

Ed looked down the road toward his place before glancing back at Amanda. "Okay," he said. "Thanks."

They walked back to the small parking lot. Amanda reached behind her seat and grabbed her purse. Leafing through, she pulled her phone out and texted Bruce while Ed was wiping some of the grime off himself: *Thanks for meeting this afternoon. I'm just thinking, do you want to get together tomorrow before you head into work for lunch? Maybe we can go for a walk.* She ended the text with a smiley face. Hoping for a response before she arrived home and went to bed, she pulled out of the parking lot and drove down Corn Neck Road. "You'll have to tell me when to turn," she said to Ed.

"I will." In fact, you can just stop at West Beach Road. I live at the end, and it can be difficult to turn around down there." He turned to Amanda. "I still can't believe I didn't see what the pond took from me. My wife knew what it took, that's for sure. She argues with me all the time. We never used to argue like that." In the dark of the car, he shook his head and sobbed out loud.

Amanda didn't know what to say or how to react, so she remained silent and let Ed express his remorse. When they reached West Beach Road, she pulled to the corner. "Remember," she said. "You can fix this."

In the soft glow of the open door, Ed nodded and left. Amanda watched him as he walked down the dirt road into the pitch darkness, then drove off hoping he'd follow her advice.

She arrived home a little after nine-thirty and checked her phone for a response from Bruce. When none showed up, she walked inside and went straight to the shower to remove the stink of Sachem Pond.

Amanda knew if she hadn't let Ed bring her into the water, she'd very likely have died from the onset of a severe asthmatic attack. She was glad to be alive, and feeling much better. Still, the possibility of losing Bruce weighed on her.

Through these emotional waves she thought about what she had told Heather earlier. She had said that she wasn't looking for a relationship; that she loved her independence; that she found more happiness returning home where no one told her how to run her days or live her life. Why then, did she feel distressed that she hadn't heard from Bruce? With these thoughts flowing through her head, she finished up in the bathroom.

Once in her bedroom she rifled through her purse for her book, *Bathing the Lion*, to try a little reading to relax, and grabbed her phone in the process. Just then a text alert went off. She let out a huge sigh and read the message from Bruce: *I'd love to meet up tomorrow. Let's chat in the AM.*

Now she could sleep without dwelling on Bruce. She leafed through the book but found herself too wired to concentrate, too charged from the day's events. Tossing the book on the nightstand, she rolled over and wrapped the quilt around her. Even though it was the middle of July, Amanda needed the weight of a blanket around her. If only Bruce were there to wrap his arms around her, maybe her life would feel complete, and safe.

But compromise was something she didn't do well. If she started a relationship with Bruce, how would she let go of the things they didn't agree about. The temperature of a room, for instance, was simply something she couldn't compromise on. Her health depended on air movement and breezes; even warm breezes were better than nothing. But now she was doing that one thing she knew she shouldn't — forecasting the future. For it was when she tried to look into the future — and began to imagine all manner of negative scenarios — that she became agitated. She remembered Heather's advice: stay in the present moment because nothing bad can happen in the present moment. That was her final thought for the night, before she dozed off.

She woke the next morning and went to the kitchen, poured a cup of coffee from the day before, and put two ice cubes in her cup. Taking a seat at the table, she glanced at her phone. The screen read eight-thirty. She sat at the table sipping her iced coffee when an alert went off telling her she had six new emails. They were all in her clients box. As she scrolled through the emails, her heart beat faster. She swept her hand through her unkempt hair. "Oh my goodness," she said. "No." Panicking now, she stood up abruptly. The chair skittered across the hardwood floor and fell on its side. Amanda ignored the chair and paced the kitchen.

147 C. Jennings Penders

Taking a deep breath, she tried to center herself. It did no good, but she went back through each email, making sure she'd read them correctly. The gist of every message was that these six clients she'd cultivated, who lived off island, were stating they were no longer in need of her services.

As Amanda read through the emails, an alert arrived telling her more mail had just come in. Afraid to open these new emails, she continued reading the previous messages again. She closed them, and then went back to see what new email had arrived. Four more off island clients were leaving her. A total of ten. She realized then that this was her entire off island base. All stated they would pay their contracts through the end of the year, but they would not be renewing. The offer to compensate her for the rest of the year was a small comfort, but not enough to keep Amanda from falling into distress. As she paced the kitchen, feeling flushed and ill, it dawned of her why this had happened: Sachem Pond had taken her livelihood in exchange for her taking from its magic!

She was dumbfounded, but then grateful. She still had all her Block Island clients, at least for now. She'd have to make every effort to keep them and look for more. It was imperative now that she go for a visit to see Tom at the Spring House.

Amanda lost her appetite as she considered again what would've happened had she not gone into Sachem Pond with Ed. She thought back to the last time she fell under a breathing attack. Had she not stayed over at Heather's place that night, she probably would not have survived that attack. Amanda played that night over again in her mind: She woke up in the middle of the night, gasping for breath—she couldn't find her voice as she stumbled into Heather's room—Heather woke up when the ceiling light came on and had a look of horror on her face while looking at Amanda struggling to breath—Heather reached for the phone and dialed 9-1-1—and shortly after, just before Amanda passed out, the emergency personnel flooded Heather's home and saved Amanda's life. Amanda shuddered while thinking about that night, and her most recent attack. Both times she'd been fortunate to be with people who could help her. As much as she relished her independence, she understood that at some point she'd need to give up some of her autonomy in favor of safety.

She stared out her window for a bit then texted Bruce.

It's 8:45. I can be ready by nine-thirty. Want to meet at Old Harbor?

Amanda tried to eat a little but she felt too ill. Her mind continued to play through the events of the previous night, and she felt sick about what her night swim had cost her. Just what would have happened had Ed not been there to help? It pained her to lose clients. But what would she do now? Too many thoughts were churning in her head and a text alert brought her out. *I can meet you by 10.*

She felt better after reading the text. It wasn't easy for her to share her life, or the challenges she faced. She'd rather help others than share her own issues. If this new friendship with Bruce was going to blossom, she'd have to neglect her old inclinations toward adamant independence.

As Amanda stepped away from the kitchen table, she thought that this might be the perfect time to connect to someone new. Perhaps Bruce could help her, even just by listening. Funny how things change, she thought. A month ago—two weeks ago even—she would never have considered a relationship with *anyone.* And now, here she was, feeling like a teenager getting ready for a first date, and already dreaming up a storybook future.

She laughed out loud at her folly as she walked to the bathroom to get ready. She rifled through her closet in the bedroom for something to wear. When she settled on a tee shirt and a pair of shorts, she went back to the kitchen, grabbed her purse, and walked out the front door. She put her sunglasses on and she drove away.

Bruce was sitting on the bench across the street from Mohegan Café when Amanda parked her Mini in the Old Harbor parking lot. "Hi, Bruce," she said, waving at him as she approached.

He rose from the bench. "I'm so glad you texted last night." He smiled and gave her a quick hug. "I don't have to work tonight until four, so we have most of the afternoon. Do you have anything in mind?"

"No. Just wanted to get together and talk." Amanda pressed her glasses back up and smiled. Her heart raced a bit as she considered her next words. She glanced at Bruce and thought back to the morning. Sighing, she shook her head. "Listen, something happened this morning that's got me rattled. I'm usually not good at sharing, but I want to start off on a good foot with you."

"What is it?" he asked. "Is everything okay?"

"I don't know." She looked down, then directly into his eyes. "I lost my off-island clients this morning. All of them. That's a loss of more than half my income, Bruce. Lost income means..." Her voice trailed. Amanda took a deep breath and expelled it. "I'm worried. I don't expect you to fix this for me, but I just wanted to tell you. If we have any chance here, we have to be honest and share what's happening in our lives." She flashed a forlorn smile and said, "I'm not good at this part of a relationship. You may have to work with me. If you think something is bothering me, and I don't tell you, continue to ask. I will get better at it."

Bruce squeezed her hand. "I might be able to help you with this. I've seen how you can turn around a business with your social media activity. That place down the street that does the past life stuff... Into the Past? I didn't even know that business existed until you spread the word." He shaded his eyes as the sun came out from behind a stray cloud. "And Michelle Joy is now busier than she ever was. You have a gift, Amanda. Maybe losing your off-island clients is a blessing. You'll have more time to spend cultivating a stronger, more lasting bond with the islanders."

She hesitated for a moment. "Maybe you're right. I do need to work with the clients I have here," she said. "I know Tom over at the Spring House has been begging me to stop by. Now I'll have time to do that. How did you know I work with Michelle?"

"I have my ways," he said, guiding Amanda away from the bench. "You feel like going for a little walk? We can talk more along the way." After he took her hand, they strolled past the Old Surf Hotel. Just past the Blue Dory Inn, Bruce led her down the beach path to the shore. He stopped in the middle of the path and said, "Are you okay with this pace?"

She took a breath. "I'm good as long as I have my inhaler if I need it. I haven't had to use it yet today. The breeze helps move the air around. As long as the air moves, even a little bit, I'm usually okay." She flashed back to the previous night and briefly considered telling Bruce about Sachem Pond, but then she held back. There were some things she just wasn't prepared to share, and the secret of the pond was something she was not supposed to reveal to anyone.

When they arrived at the beach behind the Blue Dory, Bruce held Amanda's hand and steadied her as she lowered herself to the sand. Then he took a seat beside her. "I've always liked this beach. You can look back and see downtown, and then turn back and see the ocean. The best of both worlds. And it's close enough to the National that I can come down on my fifteen-minute break if I need a beach fix. What's your favorite place on the island?"

Amanda closed her eyes and imagined North Light.

"You're there right now, aren't you?"

Opening her eyes, she laughed. "Yes indeed. North Light. It's always been my favorite place, maybe because it's so remote and takes a vehicle to get there. I love how peaceful it is. Plus, it holds a sentimental presence in my heart. My grandfather Eugene died out there. No one really knows what he was doing there in the middle of the night. I was devastated. He meant everything to me. I think that's why the lighthouse has attracted me for so long. I can always feel him when I visit. North Light was his favorite place too."

"I didn't know that." He reached out and took her hand. "Hmmm. We have more in common than I thought. As much as I enjoy being out and about surrounded by people, when I've had enough, I need to decompress. I think that may be why Block Island appeals to me. It's island life, but I still get the interaction I need. Next time we can go to North Light. How does that sound?"

"I'd like that," Amanda said, smiling. Next time? Her heart beat faster. "When I left this morning, I didn't know what to expect. I certainly wasn't looking for anything. Remember earlier I told you I'm not good at sharing?"

He nodded.

"That's not the only thing I'm not good at. I love my independence. I've gotten used to being on my own and I enjoy it. I understand a relationship, any relationship, requires compromise and I do want to see if this can work. It is nice to be here with you."

Bruce stared at Amanda. "Where did you come from?" he asked. "Do you have any clue how long I've been looking for someone compatible? I guess the old adage is true. Stop looking and what you seek will show up. I'm certainly not someone who needs lots of attention, Amanda. In fact, like you, I need downtime, and alone-time, too. Seems as if Heather knows us better than we may know ourselves." He laughed. "Are you getting hungry? You want to get some lunch?'

"I could eat."

They stood up and walked back up the Blue Dory path. "Have any place you want to go?"

Amanda pulled her phone out. She couldn't believe it said twelve-thirty. "If we stay downtown, then we don't have to rush back for you. I love the Mohegan Café."

"Okay," Bruce said. "The Mohegan it is."

When they walked in, the host smiled. "Why if it's not Bruce Pigott, the great National chef. What are you doing over here?"

"Getting lunch before I head to work," he said. "My friend Amanda said how much she loves it here."

The host stared back at the two of them. He finally found his voice. "You're Amanda Dodge."

"Right," she said, standing in the aisleway as patrons and waitstaff maneuvered around them.

"Let me show you to a table." When they were seated, the host said, "You help businesses with social media, is that correct?"

"Right," she said again.

"I'll be back in a minute," he said. "I think my manager would like to meet you."

A few minutes later, a young woman approached their table. Glancing at Amanda, she said, "I'm Helen Johnson, the manager here."

Amanda reached out to shake her hand. "Nice to see you again, Helen. I know we've never officially met, but I've seen you at some Chamber events. Our host seemed to indicate that you're looking for some social media help?"

Helen nodded. "Why don't you get your lunch? We can talk after you eat. I just wanted to come out and meet you."

All smiles now, Amanda ordered a garden burger and a bowl of clam chowder.

After they downed a couple of drinks, shared a nice long conversation, and finished eating, their waiter came by to ask about deserts, which they refused. "Very good," he said, adding, "Your lunch is on the house today, per Helen."

A little later, Helen returned.

"Thank you for lunch," Amanda said.

"You are very welcome. Can you talk for a few minutes?" she asked, sitting down between Amanda and Bruce.

"I should be heading to work," Bruce said, getting up. "We can chat later, Amanda. Yes, thank you for lunch." Helen nodded.

"How about we go to my office," Helen said after Bruce left. Amanda followed her as she stood up and walked through the restaurant. When they arrived in the office, Helen indicated a chair opposite her desk. She sat behind the desk. "How long have you known Bruce?"

"My best friend, Heather Littlefield, has worked for him as his sous chef for almost as long as he's been at the National. I guess that means over ten years."

"Hmmm..." Helen stretched her legs under the desk. "So, my host this afternoon said he thinks you can help me with my social media outreach. I'm aware that many the island businesses you've already helped have had a big jump in sales."

"You've heard about that."

"It's a small island. Word spreads."

"I'd like to if you can help us too. What's your normal fee?"

"I typically ask for an upfront deposit, and then go monthly if my clients want a trial. Or six months to a year if they are comfortable and know my track record." Amanda had learned long ago to discuss the upfront fee in the beginning of negotiations. That way when the contract fee came up, it didn't feel so threatening. "Obviously, if you opt for the longer contract you'll be charged less over the course of that contract. My upfront fee varies by the business and what their expectations are: so, my fee falls anywhere between fifteen hundred and two thousand. My month to month contract runs about three hundred a month. The six month and yearly contracts are a better deal, averaging about two hundred-fifty a month. These are flexible too. I want to keep my clients happy, and I'm not looking to rook anyone."

Helen agreed. "I like your attitude," she said. "I think we can work together. Let's firm up our plans in the next couple of days."

After Amanda stood up, she reached in her pocket and handed Helen a business card. "Call me when you want to talk further."

"Thank you. I will," she said. "Great talking today."

Amanda left Mohegan Café grinning like a schoolgirl at the site of the new cute boy in class. Not only had she secured a new client, but her first date with Bruce went so much better than she had expected. Life was good!

On her way out, she ran into Ed and his wife. Ed pulled her aside. "I am so happy I ran into you at

Sachem Pond. I took your advice and opened up to my wife. We may have lost time, but we still have our future."

"I'm so happy for you!" Amanda said, feeling genuine joy. "But what about the Pond talking something from us?"

"Well, I see it like this. If you're open to life and honest in everything you do, then magic happens, and nothing and no one can take *that* magic from you." He then smiled a big smile, took his wife's arm, and lead her into the restaurant.

As Amanda walked on, down the sidewalk, she thought Ed Ball was so very right. "Magic was everywhere on Block Island. You only had to be open to it, and let it in."

Magnetic North

T eagan Murphy woke up when she felt something granular brushing against her feet. Glancing over at the clock on her nightstand, it read five-thirty. Her right eye scraped against her pillow, and she winced. The black eye that her fiancé, Charlie Allen, had given her the day before still hurt. And I really thought I'd be Mrs. Allen soon, she thought.

But he wouldn't be causing any more damage to her, or to anyone else. Teagan made sure of that. When she reached under the covers, she felt tiny pebbles of black gravel and sand on the undersides of her feet, and on the bed sheet under the heels.

Then she recalled the dream.

In it, she had been standing at the edge of the small parking lot looking out at North Light. This marked the third time within two weeks North Light appeared in her dreams. How could I have a physical manifestation of the beach in a friggin' dream? she thought. She got out of bed and swept the sand off her feet with her hands, and then off the sheets. As she did so, she searched her memory.

An old man. She remembered an old man with a scar. He seemed to be beckoning her toward the lighthouse. But that was all she could remember from the dream.

Then she thought of North Light. The lighthouse — and the dunes around it, was her favorite place on Block Island. She planned to spend the summer there with her cousin, James Wolf. In a way, it made sense that she'd be dreaming about the lighthouse. But an old man? That was... different.

Her thoughts shifted to Charlie striking her. She was glad to discover his real nature before becoming more entangled in his web of abuse.

For now, the mystery of the old man in her dream would have to wait, as would the cause of the sand and gravel in her bed. She climbed back into bed and tried to sleep, but couldn't. It was already six o'clock, so she rolled out, stripped the bed, and threw the sheets into the washer.

While in the shower, she tried to dig up all the bits and pieces of the North Light dream. No use. Nothing else streamed in.

❖ ❖ ❖

Three days later, Teagan woke before dawn. "Damn you, Charlie," she said as she gently touched her bruised eye. Still dark at four-thirty, she fumbled for the lamp on the nightstand. When it illuminated the room, her attention was immediately drawn to a picture of North Light hanging on the wall beside her bed. Even through the pain — both the physical and emotionally draining pain — Teagan found it within herself to smile. Smiling made her feel better. For the first night this week, no dreams had invaded her sleep.

Her plans for spending the summer on the island were to begin by the end of today. Rylee, her sister, and her friend Alex, were to be the first visitors. Everyone in their circle figured Rylee and Alex would be a couple by now, but neither one seemed to get the picture. They'd been friends for years and didn't see what everyone else did — simply that they belonged together. They had what Teagan longed for but had yet to find.

At thirty-two, and successful beyond her dreams, Teagan had yet to meet Mr. Right. She thought that perhaps Charlie might be the one, before his fist connected with her face.

Teagan and Rylee operated an interior design firm called Tealee Designs. With an eye for ornate details and a great sense for color, they became quite successful. Enough so that they could summer on Block Island for as many weeks as they wished, easily able to pay the high summer rental prices. They also enjoyed the freedom of working from anywhere, and Block Island quickly became their home away from home. Teagan felt it was time to find a permanent place to stay. Fortunately, her friend and surrogate grandmother, Ester Lindstrom, offered her a place for the summer while she house-hunted on the island.

Tegan and Ester had met ten years earlier, while both were visiting North Light at the same time. Turned out, they shared an equal obsession with the lighthouse. It seemed that frequent visitors and locals all developed a need to visit a specific place on the island. For Teagan and Ester, it was North Light. It's what connected them.

Teagan needed to get away from the turmoil at the moment, and Block Island always seemed to be the best thing for her. Seeing Cousin James again certainly wouldn't hurt. She also looked forward to spending time with Ester. Not only did she consider Ester a surrogate grandmother, but almost everyone on Block Island felt the same way at one point or another. Ester was pretty much thought of as the matriarch of Block Island. She and Teagan, however, developed a strong bond, much like she and James had.

On his way from Key West in his new 120-foot Nordhavn motor yacht, James looked forward to seeing his cousin Teagan again. He spent winters in Key West and summers on Block Island, something his Uncle Chris had always dreamed of. Growing up, James heard his uncle tell him on more than one occasion how Key West and Block Island soothed his soul and felt like home. James decided to fulfill that dream for himself. His yacht, *Tapestry*, was custom built. He and his brother, Sean, had launched Wolf Gaming, a successful gaming company that provided them with the freedom to start pursing some of their dreams about seven years ago.

He and Teagan had a bond that wasn't easily broken. Being the same age and just as successful certainly helped. Neither was all that interested in having a partner to "complete them." They'd much rather find some other trouble to get into.

Being single meant they were free to take chances others may blanche at. James often enjoyed telling the story of how Teagan knocked a guy out in New Haven. He was coming onto her and no matter how many times she said no, he persisted. When Teagan had enough, she stood up and with one solid punch laid him out. "Remind me to never get on your bad side, Cuz," James had said to her that night.

❖ ❖ ❖

Teagan got out of bed and stumbled to the bathroom to get ready to meet James. She rubbed her sleep-encrusted eyes. She winced as her finger rubbed against her bruised skin. Four in the morning was no time for any civilized person to be up, she thought as she showered. When she was clothed for the day, she went to the kitchen to make her regular breakfast: a raspberry muffin with butter and a glass of lemonade. She checked her watch. Forty minutes, she thought as she washed the dishes.

She threw a raincoat in one of the bags she'd been packing the past couple of days, then zipped them up and wheeled them out to her Volkswagen Bug. Teagan had arranged for a friend to pick up her car. She didn't trust leaving it in long-term parking. Pulling out of her driveway, she grew excited about setting foot on Block Island again. It was all her Uncle Chris's fault. She often thanked him (and sometimes laughingly cursed him) for giving her this obsession with a pile of sand out in the middle of the Atlantic Ocean.

She parked her Bug, grabbed her luggage, and did a quick glance about the dock. Then she noticed the vessel *Tapestry* was arriving. Her excitement jumped up a notch.

A small crowd gathered when they saw the 120-foot yacht moving closer. *Tapestry* tended to have that effect. Seeing a private yacht of that size in New London was rarer than a white lion.

Once docked, James dashed onto the dock and embraced Teagan. "So good to see you," he said as he signaled to a staffer to grab her bags and bring them onboard. Pulling back from her, he said, "That's some shiner you have there, Teagan. What the heck happened?"

She drew in a breath and looked away. "Charlie happened. But it won't happen again. He's nursing a broken jaw, broken nose, and his smile is missing a couple of teeth."

"Sounds like you took care of him pretty good."

"He messed with the wrong person." Teagan shook her head and laughed out loud, thinking back to seeing him fall like an avalanche. "He didn't know what hit him." Suddenly, her laughter turned upside down. Tears started, and she wiped them away. "See? This is why I feel better when I'm unattached. I get involved, lower my guard, let someone in... and they always break my heart."

Teagan had a host of family and friends. Of everyone, James wound up being the only person she could be vulnerable with, probably because he carried many of the same tendencies as her. And yet, she let no one push her around. "I thought Charlie would be different. Everyone loved him. For six months he was the perfect gentleman." Her body trembled, and the tears were now streaming.

James stepped forward and embraced her again along with a few pats on the back. "Remember," he said, pulling away, focusing deeply on Teagan. "Not all guys act like that. And you're not alone in that department either. I could tell you some stories. Boy, could I tell you some stories."

She wiped the tears and a small smile appeared. "Yeah," she said. "I remember that one girl who not only stole your heart but almost stole one of your gaming company's trade secrets."

"Okay. Okay," James said, laughing now that he could laugh about it. "You're the only one who knows about that." He lowered his voice and winked. "We never bring it up in mixed company. The point is we've both had our share of miserable relationships but we've always managed to bounce back."

Now that Teagan had vented, she looked around the yacht. "Hmmm," she said. "This is *quite* impressive. It's almost as big as the ferry boats! I think Uncle Chris would be thrilled for you, and probably a little bit envious."

"Come on," he said, gesturing with his arm for her to join him. "Let me give you the grand tour."

After marveling at the size of the salon, which was easily twice the size of any living room she'd ever been in, James lead Teagan down the lower-deck passageway, past a few cabins sporting queenside berths, he opened the door to a darken cabin and waved Teagan inside. After he switched on a light, Teagan saw something that blew her away. An entire bulkhead was taken up with a golf simulator. She looked back at James as her jaw dropped. She could only stare and point at the screen.

"I know," James said. "But I love my golf. Always have."

Teagan couldn't believe the scope of the cabin. She finally found her voice and said, "If I loved golf as much as you do, I'd never leave this room."

"It ain't easy," James said, smiling. "There's much more to see, but I wanted to show this cabin first. We have about a forty-minute ride to Block Island"

"I can't wait to get there."

"I know how you feel."

"By the way, I've been wondering, what's with the name, *Tapestry*?"

"Tapestry. As in a woven tapestry. Pull on a thread and everything changes." He smiled. "And it's the title of one of my favorite Star Trek Next Generation episodes. Season six, episode fifteen."

Teagen laughed. "You know the episode number?"

"You know I'm a huge Star Trek fan."

"Isn't that the episode where Picard learns through Q that had he not taken risks as a brazen young man he never would have been captain of the Enterprise?"

"Yup. That's it."

"You made me watch that show all the time when we were visiting Uncle Chris. The two of you knew all the dialogue between characters. Can I now tell you how annoying that was?"

James laughed. "I know I've made you watch more than your fair share." He walked over to a rocking chair and sat down, gesturing to the chair beside him. Teagan put her feet up while James stretched out. "That episode, *Tapestry,* is about what happens if we change one event in our lives. Like Uncle Chris, I believe that if we could change one event, no matter how insignificant, that one change would have ramifications throughout the rest of our lives. It's the moral of the *Tapestry* episode. Don't mess with your timeline and destiny." He took a breath, rocked forward, and stood up. "Shall we move on? I want to show you more of the boat before we get to the island."

As they walked through the boat, James pointed out his master stateroom. "I have three guest rooms too."

When Teagan passed a window, she glanced back at James. "We must be getting close to the island. Can we step outside? I need to see North Light the moment it comes into view."

"I forgot how obsessed you are with that place," he said, shaking his head as he walked her to a bulkhead door. Guiding her through, they stepped onto the starboard deck and he said, "Here ya go. We should see Sandy Point, the north tip of Block Island, shortly."

She smiled and did her little happy dance. It had been two years since she visited North Light. Closing her eyes, she envisioned herself sitting there and felt excited all over again. This summer, she planned on doing some of her work at the beach, on her laptop.

Teagan leaned over the railing as North Light came into view. Then, in an instant, her balance and vision went askew. She pressed her eyes closed, then opened them. "What... what's happening?" Teagan asked. She looked over at James and said, "Something's not..."

Pulling her away from the railing, James said, "Are you alright?"

"Something's not..." Her voice drifted off as she slumped, slipped away from James, and fell backward, hitting her head on the deck.

❖ ❖ ❖

The old man took a breath and looked out at the long trek he had in front of him. Would he make it? He stood in the small parking lot at the terminus of Corn Neck Road and looked at the distant North Light. The structure, tiny at that distance, was illuminated by the moonlight. Even as a young man, the walk along the stony beach was a struggle. This time, Eugene knew he wouldn't make it back. His health was failing fast, and he wanted to pass on Block Island, at his favorite place: North Light. In the gathering darkness, he began his last walk to the lighthouse. Even with the full moon shining off the Atlantic Ocean, and bouncing reflections off the sand, Eugene could clearly see where he was walking. He was prepared though; he pulled the small flashlight from his pocket and switching it on.

Not too far into his trek to the lighthouse, he felt his breath begin to fade and shortly thereafter he fell to the sand. Suffering from congestive heart failure and having had two heart attacks in the past five years, he knew what was happening. He sat in the sand and took several shallow breaths. Suddenly feeling a presence behind him, he turned back to see a young woman approaching.

"Teagan?" he inquired. "Where's James?"

Startled, Teagan stared back at the old man. "How do you know my name? Who are you? How do you know my cousin?" Eugene remained seated on the cool sand, silent. That's when she noticed the scar on the right side of his face, running from just below his eye to the edge of his jaw. She looked away but apparently not quickly enough. "You're from my dream."

"Yes," he said. "Look at the scar. Everyone does. And everyone has them. Some are visible, some aren't." He grew quiet then and realized something was amiss. "Oh no." The old man felt more of his life drain away. "I *thought* this time when I saw you it was real. I need to ask, why do you keep returning? And why have you invaded my experience?"

"Your experience?" Teagan asked. "If anything, you've invaded my experience. You came to me."

Tears ran down his face. He turned back to face his initial destination, North Light. He almost as if he'd woken from a trance when Teagan arrived, only to fall back into it again. He regained his strength, stood up, and continued on his final journey. No matter how many times Teagan attempted to engage the old man, he either ignored her or hadn't realized she was walking beside him.

"Wait!" she shouted. "What do you mean you thought this was real?" Eugene kept moving forward, more determined than ever to stop this crazy loop in time. He didn't know for sure why he was here, or what event, if any, he was supposed to stop. Every time he came close to discovering why Teagan came to him, he found himself back at this beach, returning to North Light.

His legs grew weaker, his breath shallower but Eugene kept moving forward, slower now, but with more purpose. He grinned as he came upon the natural walkway of sand to the lighthouse. Beach plum bushes lined the path, and a memory of a little girl came to mind. It was August, and they were running to the lighthouse. As they raced, time slowed down. A small laugh, her little sailor's dress swaying around her. Her long wavy hair bounced with each step. Teagan raced up beside the old man before he vanished around the corner, and asked, "Who are you?" The little girl struggled to breath. Before he could pick her up to carry her, she disappeared.

Ignoring her, he looked ahead and saw the flagpole and salvation. "I'm gonna make it! I'm gonna make it!" He laughed out loud. It was the first time he heard himself laugh in months, and that brought about more laughter mixed with bittersweet tears. He'd miss all this, but he knew he'd be back.

Somehow the old man found a burst of energy. Teagan made her best attempt to keep up. She wanted to figure out how Eugene knew her.

A few years prior to his first heart attack, Eugene had gone to a hypnotist for a past life regression session. He discovered that he'd lived on Block Island

171 C. Jennings Penders

before as a member of the Dodge family, years ago. Not long after, he found that he always returned to the Dodge family and even found the gravestone from his previous life.

Further research verified he was indeed the person interred. He had no fear of dying, he just didn't want to suffer. Being at North Light upon his passing would be the most pleasant place he could be.

For what would be the final time, he sat down along the main path. It took him longer to move now. He lay back in the sand, gathering his last breaths. They were coming slower now, and his heartbeat slowed to gradual intervals. Then a sharp pain ran down his right arm. Waiting for the pain to pass, he took several quick short breaths. He heard the pitter patter of little feet in the sand. Then a little girl ran past him. After several minutes, Eugene got to his feet, stumbled along the path, and walked the last fifty feet to the lighthouse. All the while, he called out for Amanda.

As Teagan drew closer, she heard the old man calling out and wondered who Amanda was.

Growing more desperate, Eugene finally collapsed at the foot of North Light. Wrapping his arms around the building in a loving embrace, he called for Amanda one final time. Then with a serene smile and a tear in his eye, he passed into eternity.

❖ ❖ ❖

Teagan's eyes fluttered open for a moment, and then closed again. Opened and closed, attempting to focus on something. "What happened?" she asked, trying to sit up. That's when she found herself in a bed. She immediately fell back, still disoriented from the experience of blacking out. "What am I doing in my bed?" Then as her vision cleared, she realized she didn't recognize anything in this room. Where am I? I followed this old man—Eugene!—to North Light—and saw him die.

"North Light again, huh?"

"What's the tone for?" Teagan asked. As her mind cleared, she understood she must be in one of the guest cabins on *Tapestry*.

"Just seems you're obsessed with that place. Could it be you were simply..." James paused a moment when he realized that what he wanted to say turned out to be the exact wrong word. Tell her she was dreaming would only set her off. As he considered to moment, he understood that she couldn't be dreaming. She had blacked out she had not gone to sleep.

"What are you talking about?" She swung her legs over the edge of the bed before she realized she didn't feel right. She lay back down to gather her strength. Then she sat up again and once more brought her feet to the carpet. Taking several breaths, she stood up and said, "Eugene."

"Who's Eugene?" James asked.

173 C. Jennings Penders

"An old man who seems to know us. He asked where you were, he knew our names. I watched him die at the lighthouse." Confused by the events, Teagan decided she had to know what happened to Eugene. "I need to find out who this old man is, or was. Will you help me?"

"And do exactly what if we find him?" James glanced out at the bluffs of Clay Head just before the captain piloted *Tapestry* into Old Harbor, and toward Ballard's special dock that was waiting for them, the only dock that could hold a 120-foot power yacht.

"I don't know. Hopefully we can discover why he died there all alone."

"You *know* we can't change the past, Teagan," James said, tilting his head. "Even says so in lettering right under the name of my boat." Seeing her standing without assistance made him feel better. "You had me worried." He cleared his throat. "When you hit your head on the deck, I thought for sure you'd have a melon on your head. But you don't even have a scratch. I'm hoping there's no concussion. Are you feeling alright?"

"Yes, I'm fine," Teagan said. "Can we go back upstairs?"

"You mean above deck? Sure."

James led Teagen to the top deck of *Tapestry* just as the crew was tying the vessel to the dock cleats and the captain was shutting down the engines. When she looked to the northwest across Old Harbor and saw the National Hotel—in all its splendor—poking up behind the docked ferry boats, a broad smile turned to gleeful laughter. She clapped and spun around, cheering for the island. She was home!

Just like when *Tapestry* approached New London, heads turned, and a small crowd gathered at Old Harbor to gesture at the size of the yacht. Teagan looked down at the gawkers and again about what had happened after she'd fallen and passed out. She couldn't shake the feeling that Eugene was a real person who died alone at North Light. Why had he appeared in her mind when the was blacked out? For what purpose? And how did he know her cousin James?

James broke her thoughts when he suggested they go ashore for something to eat. "Don't know about you, Teagan, but I'm headed to Finn's for my fried clams."

She joined him and they stepped off the vessel onto the dock and walked past several people standing nearby, on the sandy area in front of Ballard's Inn, looking at *Tapestry*.

"Saw you come in," a young woman said while removing her sunglasses. She smiled at James as he strolled past her. "That's quite a boat you have out there. What is it? One-hundred feet?"

"One-hundred twenty," he said, pausing in his stride. "Not too far off."

"I'm Rebecca Rose," the woman said, extending a hand.

"James Wolf," he said, shaking it.

She grew quiet for a moment, then said, "Any relation to Sean Wolf"

"My brother. How do you know him?"

Teagan watched the conversation unfold, feeling left out. She tapped James on the shoulder. "Think I'll head to Ester's and grab my Jeep. We can meet up at Finn's," she said.

James slapped his forehead. "Oh, gee. I'm sorry. This is my cousin, Teagan Murphy."

"Hi Teagan." They also shook hands.

"Nice to meet you, Rebecca," Teagan said, and she watched Rebecca visibly relax after hearing what their relationship was. Rebecca's fists unclenched and she let out a long exhale. Teagan couldn't help but laugh out loud as they exchanged nods.

"What's so funny?" James asked. "Are you sure you're okay to walk to Ester's?"

"Sorry. I don't know why I laughed. I'll be fine. Ester's isn't far from here," Teagan said. "You enjoy your conversation and I'll meet up with you at Finn's in a bit."

Teagen turned and made her way along the dock.

After a long pause James said to Rebecca, "I'll be right back." He then chased after Teagan.

Rebecca smiled. "I'll be right here!" she shouted after him.

Catching up with Teagan he said, "We're out of earshot. Now what's so funny?"

"You didn't see it?" Teagan said.

"See what?"

"That woman likes you. When she thought we were together, her entire body tightened up as she was protecting herself from heartbreak. I watched it happen."

"That's silly," James said, shaking his head.

"Why did she stop you like that? You know, that's what usually happens when people see us together. You probably have missed out on twenty dates because of it. I just never noticed how well it works and her expression made me laugh and holy..." She left the last word unspoken. "You've got to admit that's funny."

James couldn't help but chuckle too. "Maybe we should start wearing shirts that say 'Just Cousins' from now on whenever we're hanging out in public." Teagan grimaced. "I wouldn't have it any other way. I'll be at Finn's by four. We can meet up then."

"Sure."

Teagan walked toward downtown, leaving James to return to Rebecca. With the summer in bloom, tourists and islanders alike congregated outside the shops and pubs. Star Department Store was especially busy. A line started at the front door and snaked outside. She managed to work her way through the crowds and continued through the downtown district. Passing the Empire movie theater and Malcolm Greenaway's studio, the sidewalks along Spring Street became less crowded. She passed the 1661 Inn and finally arrived at Spring House driveway.

She stopped at the edge of the driveway debating whether or not to go up and see Sean. She decided against it. He would only ask her about her black eye and she didn't feel like telling that story yet again.

Teagan focused on the road and tried to clear her mind. This downhill portion of Spring Street and the two sharp bends in the road ahead were a little treacherous. Not only did the steepness surprise people, but the speed of bikers and drivers made stopping somewhat challenging.

Teenagers, thinking they were indestructible, took too many chances—not only here—but all over the island. Teagan recalled being a teenager herself, and she had taken plenty of chances herself, some that others would never have dream of. Sometimes she still did.

She stopped at the side of the road to let four or five bikers continue on their reckless ride. When they had traveled a safe distance, Teagan walked on. After a bend in the road, she took a right down a long dirt driveway, which rose up slowly as it revealed a hill upon which sat a cedar-shingled house and wraparound porch. There was a three car, unattached garage off to the left of the house. As she had expected, Ester was sitting on the porch looking out at the water, waiting for her favorite guest.

She stood up and waved as Teagan made her way across the lawn. When close enough, Ester said, "My gosh, it's been too long." She moved with the ease of someone fifteen years younger as she bounded down the three steps. "Let me look at you." She took both of Teagan's hands and held them out. "Oooh. Sweetie, are you alright?"

Had this been the first time Teagan heard her speak, she'd have immediately recognized the Scandinavian accent. However, having known Ester for over a decade, she no longer noticed the accent.

Ester's hair was jet black, almost Mediterranean looking in color and coarseness. Ester's Swedish family could pass for anything other than Scandinavian.

"It's great to see you too, Ester. And you're right. It has been too long. The black eye's a story for another day. I've come to get my Jeep, so I can get my bags off James' yacht. You should see the size of this thing!"

"Is that the big boat I saw coming in just a while ago?"

"That was probably it. It's almost the size of a ferry."

"Then I saw it. The Jeep is in the garage. I drive it once or twice a month just like you asked me to. Do you still have your house key?"

"Yes indeed. Attached right here," Teagan said, fishing in her pocket for her key chain. "I'm so happy to be here, Ester. In fact, I think it's time I start looking for my own place. Rylee and I have discussed it, but we haven't moved forward. She drags her feet on the idea, but I'm not waiting on her any longer."

"I'm so happy to have some special time with you this summer, Teagan. Having you here is always a blessing."

Smiling now, Teagan said, "I know that. And thank you. I certainly plan on staying with you through the summer. Still need a place of my own, though. Sorry to cut this so short but James is waiting for me at Finn's." She gave Ester another squeeze. "When I get back later, I have a mystery I want to run by you. Something I think you can help me with."

"Looking forward to hearing all about it."

Then she walked to the three-car garage. Stepping inside, she found her Jeep with a full tank of gas. "I'll be back soon," she shouted as she drove out of the driveway. "And thank for filling the tank!"

Ester smiled and waved when Teagan drove off.

When she arrived back in town, she parked as close to the dock as possible, in the small parking area out front of Ballard's that few tourists knew about. She walked down the dock to *Tapestry*, and went aboard. One of the crewmembers help her gather her bags and loaded them into her jeep.

When she looked around before driving up to park near Finn's to meet James, she spotted a couple on the other side of the breaker that ran along Ballard's large outdoor patio. The couple was sitting side-by-side on the sand, facing the sea. She'd recognize the back of that head anywhere. She locked the Jeep and strolled up to the couple.

"You too have been talking all this time?"

"Oh, hi cuz," James said and then thought to look at his wristwatch. "It's really three-thirty already?"

"Yup," Rebecca said. "I guess you weren't so hungry for clams after all. I was rushing because I expected you to be waiting for me at Finn's."

Rebecca grimaced and said, "Sorry. We got to talking."

"That's okay," Teagan said.

"Well, I should let you go," Rebecca said to James, and stood up, brushing the sand of her capri shorts. He got to his feet also. "You have my number, so feel free to call anytime. Great to finally meet you and talk with you, James." She gave him a hug. "And Teagan, I'm sorry we slighted you."

Teagan gave a slight wave and said, "Don't worry about it. Like I said, we're only cousins. And it gave me the chance to see Ester sooner than I had expected, and to get my Jeep from her garage. Besides, I understand the desire to chat away when meeting someone new."

As they walked away from the beach, Teagan glanced at James. "So," she said, waiting for her cousin to fill her in. He didn't budge.

Taking the hint, Teagan remained quiet while they walked toward Finn's restaurant.

"Nothing much changes here, does it?" James finally said, looking around. "Ernie's Old Harbor Restaurant. Star Department Store. The bike and auto rentals. Ballard's, of course. Some things change, but for the most part the island feels like it's frozen in time. I think that's why I still love it here. Ever since college I never imagined I could settle in one place. That's why I wanted *Tapestry*. It's mobile. I can move around as much as I want. Being here now though, even for this short time, I think I understand what Sean sees in this place."

"Could your new-found interest in Block Island have anything to do with meeting fresh-faced Rebecca today?"

He continued to ignore her prodding about Rebecca. "I'm not saying I'm staying. But to be honest, as we navigated up the coast, I couldn't help but think about you, Sean, and Rylee... and how much I've missed. And you guys aren't the only ones on Block Island. I have friends here too that I miss." James stepped on the deck of Finn's. "Gary here at Finn's for example. You know how Sean has Tom at the Spring House, well, Gary has been my good friend for years now. You have Ester. And Rylee? Well, I think she's too invested in Alex to think about anyone else."

James shouted inside Finn's when he arrived at the takeout window. James smiled at Teagan. "Hey, Gary! Can we order two fried clams and two sides of French fries with vinegar?"

"Be right with you." Then recognizing the voice, Gary dropped what he was doing and stepped outside. "James! Teagan! When did you guys arrive?"

"Late morning," Teagan said. "So happy to be home again.

"Well, it's wonderful to see you." He then turned to James. "Have you stopped in to see your brother yet?"

"We'll head over there after we eat."

They sat and waited for their meal, which Gary brought out to them himself. "Lots of vinegar on the fries, just the way you like them," Gary said, handing one tray to James and the second one to Teagan.

A line of hungry patrons began to form on the deck. "Looks like I won't be able to talk now. Can't wait to catch up later." With that said, Gary walked back to the kitchen.

Once they both finished, James brought both trays to the order window. Then he returned to the table. "Alright then," he said, moving away from the table. "Are you ready to move on?" They stepped off the deck. James started to walk to the Spring House when Teagan stopped him.

"Remember, I have my Jeep?"

"Oh, that's right. Well, why don't you get your Jeep? I'll go see Sean."

With that decided, they went in opposite directions, Teagan back downtown and James continuing to the Spring House. She watched him for a moment, hoping truly that nothing so challenging would confront her cousin. They learned not to press each other. When James was ready, he'd talk. To her before anyone else. Once she could no longer see him, Teagan continued walking back to get her Jeep.

James came to the driveway that led to the Spring House. He stood at the bottom of the hill and looked up the driveway hesitating for a moment, he finally blew out his long-held breath and decided to walk up the drive.

As Teagan passed by the Spring House on her way back to Ester's, she couldn't help but wonder about James. She was not worried per se, more curious. She felt an overwhelming desire to pull up and discover the issue that took such air out of everyone. This wasn't a one-punch-and-you're-out disturbance at a local bar. This was something more drawn out. But then she thought that may be blowing everything out of proportion.

Teagan drove on. At that bend in the road, she took that anonymous right. And there, Ester sat on the front porch in her favorite chair.

Teagan turned the Jeep around in the field just before the three-car garage and slowly backed it in. Another piece of important information her Uncle Chris imparted on her: It's always easier to see the road when it's right in front of you than when it's behind you. Much like the past.

She stepped out grabbing one bag to start unloading and strolled across the lawn. The view was so pretty it stopped her in her tracks. From where she stood, Teagan could see the wide expanse of the ocean in front of her. If she remained quiet, she heard the waves lapping the shore. No wonder Ester loved it here so much, Teagan thought as she continued her trek to the porch.

"I'm about to fix us dinner. How does wild salmon, asparagus, and mashed potatoes sound?" Ester stood up and moved away from her rocking chair.

"I can taste it already."

"I remember how much you love salmon. Did I ever tell you fish was a staple when I grew up in Sweden?" she said, opening her front door. Teagan followed her inside. "Living in a small fishing community, how could it not be? I remember pickled herring." She made a stink face. "Oooh... those first few bites. Surprisingly, I actually started to like it. I still make it now and then. It brings me right back to Sweden." Ester looked out the kitchen window and surveyed her land. "Block Island is my home now, but so much of this reminds me of Sweden. That's why I settled here."

Like Block Island now, the crowds swelled in her hometown in Sweden each summer, and she told stories about the tourist-crowded streets, and how business was good for her and her family. She started visiting Block Island in the early 1950s with her husband, Hoffy. In 1959, for a mere $5,000, they bought this small place of their own on a fourteen-acre plot, and they became part of the year-round island community. One the biggest changes she and Hoffy made to the house was the wraparound porch they added, right after they had moved in.

Not long after that, Hoffy became ill. He felt blessed to have had a least a couple years on the island before his health took a turn. He passed a year and half later, and Ester found herself even more embraced by the empathy and kindness of the islanders.

When she would walk through the downtown area, people she didn't know would stop her on the street and ask how she was doing. Ester felt more loved here than anywhere she had ever lived. Now, after all this time, she felt even more comfortable, and more at home.

Teagan knew all of this. She had heard Esther's stories over the course of their familial friendship.

"Can I help you do anything?" Tegan asked, after putting her bags in her bedroom.

Ester grabbed a few things from the refrigerator. "I'm good. While I prepare dinner, why don't you talk to me about this mystery you need help with? And when you're ready, I want to know what happened to that eye of yours as well."

Teagan walked over and moved a barstool away from the counter that separated the kitchen from the dining area. Sitting down and continuing to ignore Ester's query about her black eye, Teagan explained what had happened on the way over to the island that morning. "So, as we passed North Light, I blacked out. While unconscious I witnessed an old man walking to the lighthouse to die."

Ester stopped working and stared at Teagan. "Alright," she said. "We'll table the black eye for now. But you're going to tell me what happened. So, this old man, did he have a scar running down his face?"

"Yes! How did you know?"

"His name is Eugene Dodge," Ester said, returning to preparing dinner. "As in Dodge Street. One of the original families to settle here. His granddaughter, Amanda, still lives here."

Teagan lurched at Amanda's name. "That's the person he was looking for! He kept calling her name."

Ester went to the stove. After placing the salmon and asparagus inside the oven, she sat down beside Teagan and continued telling what she knew. "Well, there's your answer, Teagan." Ester waited to see if she could connect the dots.

"You think I'm supposed to find Amanda and connect them?"

"That's exactly what I think," Ester said. "We have a running start, however. I know Amanda quite well. I will talk to her tomorrow."

"Is there anyone you don't know on this island?" Teagan asked, all the while understanding the answer would surprise her either way.

A knock at the front door startled them both. "Anyone home?"

"James!" Ester said. "It's great to see you. C'mon in." She stood aside as he walked in. "Been way too long. Teagan talks about you every time she visits. I just put dinner in the oven, salmon and asparagus. Are you interested? There's plenty."

"Sounds delicious," he said, taking the last barstool. "Thank you."

"Great. We'll have ourselves a dinner party then. Will you set the table? Plates are in this cabinet here." Ester nodded to the cabinet closest to the oven. "Glasses are right next to it. Silverware is in the drawer below."

"All right," said James.

"Teagan and I were just discussing her blackout on her way over this morning. Very scary."

"Yes. She certainly gave me a fright," he said, eyeing Teagan.

"And she started to tell me about Eugene Dodge. I believe you know his granddaughter, Amanda."

"Yes, I do. We've met here and there. Seems like a nice girl."

"I could call her if you'd like. We could have breakfast here tomorrow. Then you can lay out your story," Ester suggested.

"Maybe," Teagan sighed.

At the end of dinner Teagan scraped the last of the salmon and asparagus onto her fork and shoveled it into her mouth. "That tasted so amazing, Ester. Thank you for cooking."

Ester moved around the table, collecting the dirty plates and silverware. "You both go sit down. I'll clean up. And you're welcome. I love to cook, especially when I have appreciative guests. Oh, and James? You're welcome to stay here tonight. That way Teagan and I can fill you in on what we've learned about her blackout this afternoon."

James and Teagan went into the living room and continued their conversation. "You know you can't change what happened? Right, Teagan?"

"I think we can. And I'm going to try."

He learned a long time ago not to try to steer Teagan. She was in full command of her own course in life. Both of them being so similar, James realized that challenging her in any way would only make her dig in deeper.

"So how do you think you can help?" he asked.

Curling into the couch and pulling at a frayed string on her tank top, Teagan said, "When Eugene arrived at the lighthouse, he kept calling for Amanda. I think she planned on meeting him there, but obviously didn't make it. I'm guessing if I can make that connection... make that meeting happen... it will end this cycle. Then Eugene can move forward."

James sighed in exasperation. "All good points. But you don't even know if Amanda will be willing to help."

"And I won't unless I talk to her in the morning. Let's talk about something else. I've decided to look for a place. Somewhere to call home on the island. I don't know what your plans are but I started to think that we could get more bang for our buck if we pooled our resources and maybe get a duplex or some shared property. I know we don't necessarily have to worry about pooling our resources. Just kinda thought since we get along so well together..." She left the rest of the thought go unsaid.

He grew quiet for a moment, considering the gesture. "Yeah," he finally said. "I like it. Let's talk more about it tomorrow." He looked at his watch. "I'm getting a little sleepy. Think I might call it a night. I'll come back in the morning for breakfast. Maybe Ester will make some of her famous Swedish pancakes. See you all in the morning."

Teagan and Ester stayed up, talking, for a while longer, but by nine they were both shutting down. Neither were able to keep their eyes open.

Teagan sat up. "I'm headed to bed, Ester." She uncurled herself from the cozy sofa to head to her even cozier bed at Ester's.

Left alone, Ester smiled and thought about how nice it felt to have company in the house again. Even though like Teagan—she appreciated her solitude—Ester still enjoyed when her home was filled with friends. Yawning, she realized she needed sleep as well. She crept up to her room and was asleep before ten.

Ester woke at five-thirty, and moved about the house quietly so as to not wake up Teagan. She got her morning paper and began to make Swedish pancakes— Teagan's favorite. She moved easily around the kitchen, almost as if she could do everything with her eyes closed. Sometimes she did. On several occasion, while her hands were making magic, she frequently found herself back in her sister's bakery in Sweden with her sister right beside her. The two of them baking. That's when Ester knew the same charm that flowed through her village in Sweden had followed her to Block Island—as much if not more than she ever experienced in Sweden. Using the family recipe was the only thing that gave her such a keen sense of nostalgia. With the batter mix complete, she sat in the dining area and watched the sky brighten as the sun rose higher in the sky.

Ester sat down at the kitchen table with her cup of coffee and leafed through the newspaper. Turning around to see the time, six-forty-five, she considered calling Amanda. Ester knew she'd be up by now because they pretty much kept the same schedule. Amanda usually got up early to catch the sunrise on film. Ester got up because she could never sleep past six. She picked up her phone and fiddled with it several times, but finally she decided to wait until at least eight. Meanwhile, she continued reading the newspaper.

By nine-thirty Amanda ambled up the porch steps and joined Ester at the table for pancakes. "So," she said, taking a sip of black coffee, "you said you have news about Eugene?"

"Do you know Teagan and Rylee Murphy?"

"Can't say that I do. Should I?"

"They are cousins to Sean and James Wolf. Anyway, Teagan arrived yesterday, and she had an experience I think you'd like to hear about. She should be up in a few." Ester adjusted her position and looked out a kitchen window. An osprey flew by with a wiggling fish in its talons. "See?" she said. "This is why I love living here. You never get tired of seeing nature in all its glory." She turned back to the conversation at hand.

Just then, Ester heard knocking on her front door. "James? Is that you?"

"It is," he said. He opened the door and walked inside. He carried a travel mug, presumably with coffee. "You must be Amanda Dodge," he said taking a seat at the table and putting the cup down.

She smiled and held out her hand. "I am," she said.

"Has Ester filled you in?" James asked, sipping from the coffee and smiling at Ester. "You do understand that there's no changing what happened. You can't change the past. And you can't change Eugene's passing."

"What's he talking about?" Amanda asked.

"Were you supposed to meet Eugene the night he went to North Light?"

She looked away and drew in a breath. She started to cry. Amanda was close to her grandfather and his passing was still an open wound. "I went to the mainland on urgent business. I had no time to let my grandfather know."

Ester took her hand. "We think your grandfather is stuck in a loop because he needs to say goodbye to you. I think Teagan can help you. She's always had an obsession for North Light, and we know Eugene did as well. Not to mention you spend quite a bit of time at that lighthouse too."

Teagan came into the kitchen rubbing her eyes. "Morning," she said, helping herself to a cup of coffee. "Let me guess, you're Amanda?"

Amanda nodded. "Ester thinks you can help me."

Taking a sip of coffee, Teagan said, "I hope this doesn't sound weird, but…your grandfather seems to have attached himself to me for some reason. Maybe he doesn't even know why. I'm guessing he doesn't. But whatever the case, that's where we're at."

Amanda sipped from her coffee. "How do you think you can help?"

Teagan shared her story again finishing with, "I think your grandfather expected to see you at the lighthouse and when you didn't show, he simply gave up and passed without saying goodbye."

"My grandfather loved Block Island and loved North Light more. That's why he lived at Golden Grove. He could see the lighthouse from everywhere at that place. I think his favorite pastime was sitting out on his porch. In one direction he could see North Light and in the other he had the ferries. Wiping the tears away, she said, "And now he's gone." Ester squeezed Amanda's hand. "How about we go to North Light."

"I'll say it again," James said, shaking his head. "You can't change the past. You're going on a fool's errand."

"I don't think we are," Amanda said. "We're not changing the past. My grandfather is already dead.

How can we change that? Unless you know where the fountain of youth is, there's no way we can bring him back." She picked up her coffee cup and took the last sip. "No," she said, putting the empty cup back on the table. "The only thing I want is to say goodbye to my grandfather. You can come with us or stay here. Teagan and I are going."

Ester moved away from the table. "If you're going to North Light, you'll need some sustenance. Let me make some sandwiches."

As Ester got busy with lunch, Teagan and Amanda cleared the breakfast table. James helped Ester.

"Will you go to that closet there?" Ester asked James, pointing to the door on the other side of the kitchen. "Should be a green cooler in there." With the food prepared and put in the cooler, James brought it out to Amanda's car.

It was around eleven o'clock when Teagan and Amanda drove away. They made it to Dodge street pretty quickly. Teagan looked over at Amanda. Pointing out the sign, she said, "So this street is really named after your family?"

Turning red from slight embarrassment but also a bit of pride, Amanda smiled. "Yes, indeed. My grandfather traced the history at some point. Fascinating stuff. Eugene's father, Tristram, named after one of the original settlers of Block Island, didn't keep the name when introducing himself, especially once he started school. Teased mercilessly the first few times he did, Tristram learned quickly and started going by Tim."

Amanda turned right on Corn Neck Road, passing Diamond Blue Surf Shop. She continued past State Beach. "My grandfather told me that later, once his father graduated from high school, he kind of regretted not standing up for himself and explaining why the name Tristram was an important part of Block Island history. He stopped using Tim and went back to Tristram." Taking her eyes off the road for a brief moment, Amanda glanced at Teagan.

"So. If you don't mind me asking, what's with the black eye?"

Silence.

"Ya know, sometimes it's easier to talk to a complete stranger. Someone who holds no preconceived notions. Someone who knows nothing about us."

Watching out the passenger side window as the scenery changed from beach to wooded area, a forlorn smile on her face, Teagan began. "Charlie. We were dating for six months and he was the kindest soul. My family loved him. I *thought* I loved him. Then everything changed. It started out as verbal abuse because he thought I cheated on him. And he kept on it. No matter how many times I told him I didn't, he refused to believe me. And that's when this happened." Teagan pointed to her eye. "The one and only and last time he became physical with me." With a stronger smile now, Teagan said, "Charlie didn't know what hit him. He spent the afternoon in the hospital and got lucky that I didn't press charges. He'll think twice before going after anyone else. At least I hope so."

"Impressive," Amanda said. A moment later, the hidden road for Golden Grove appeared on the right. As she passed the dirt driveway, Amanda glanced over at Teagan. "Hey," she said, "with my grandfather gone now, we're going to need someone to watch over Golden Grove. Would you be interested? Ester told me that you're looking for a place. Perhaps we can satisfy two needs?"

Teagan thought it over. After a bit of inner reflection, she said, "I'd like that. Thank you."

"Alright," Amanda said. "Glad that's settled. I started to worry about who I could find and trust on such short notice."

A few moments later, they were parking in the small parking lot in front of Sachem Pond. North Light was just ahead, as was a possible ghostly reunion.

Amanda stepped out of the car and looked back at Sachem Pond. Thinking again how much mystery and magic really happened here on Block Island gave her a chill. The healing pond, and now a meeting with her dead grandfather? If she told these stories to anyone else, they'd probably lock her up in a padded room. "Are you coming?"

Teagan jumped out and the two of them started walking toward North Light. "Doesn't feel right," she said. "Something's missing." That's when Teagan heard

Eugene's voice. She couldn't see him, but she heard that voice in her head.

"Where's your cousin?" Then in a trembling voice, Eugene said, "Is… is that Amanda?"

Amanda gave no indication that she heard him. She continued hiking toward North Light.

"Whoa!" Teagan said, racing after her. "Slow down, Amanda. I figured out what's missing. Eugene can't see you until we get James here."

"But he won't help, remember?"

"I don't think he needs to help. I think he just needs to be here. You know, like a counterweight, a balance." Teagan caught up to Amanda just as she approached the path to the lighthouse. "James doesn't even have to believe us. I remember Eugene asking where James was. Just now, he asked where my cousin was. So, see? He needs James here."

Amanda hung her head down low and sighed. Her voice trembling, she said, "Mm… maybe we should head back."

They began heading back down the beach. When they reached the parking lot, she leaned against her car. She placed her hands on the hood and looked up at Teagan as tears streamed down her face. "My grandfather meant everything to me. I wanted to be here that night." She wiped the tears away with the backs of her hands. "I tried to get back. But I missed the ferry. When I found out he was gone I felt devastated." She looked away, shaking her head. A shudder. Then another one. Amanda broke down. "I... I can't... I can't believe he's gone. These past two months feel like it's been twenty years."

Teagan felt Amanda's pain. She moved to stand beside her. "I understand how much Eugene meant to you. My uncle introduced me to Block Island and because of that, I've made a whole new family out here. Maybe we can't reunite you with your grandfather, but I'm not giving up." She reached out and hugged Amanda. "We should eat something. Ester made us some food." Teagan walked to the back of Amanda's car just as a Block Island taxi pulled into the parking lot.

Ester and James stepped out, and James was carrying a bag from Finn's.

"I finally convinced him he needs to be here," Ester said, walking James over to Teagan. "Let's all eat before we figure out our next step."

They sat on a group of large rocks on the beach, just off the parking lot. James opened the Finn's bag and took out a fish sandwich and French fries for Ester. Then he unpacked a lobster and crab salad, a plastic bowl of New England clam chowder, and a cup of water with lemon for himself. As he started to eat... but... something shifted.

Day became dusk.

An old man, presumably Eugene, came out of the darkness. He appeared next to James and reached out, putting his hand on James' shoulder. Eugene looked at James, as if to say something with his eyes, and then turned his head to face North Light. "You're the counterweight, James. But you're also the impetus. I thought you just needed to be here," Eugene said. "But I realized after listening to Amanda and Teagan that you don't believe you can help us. That by helping you'll mess with the fabric of our lives. Is that true? You don't believe you can help us?"

Silence.

"Let me show you it isn't true." Eugene started walking toward North Light. The sky was still hovering with the odd darkness. He looked back at James. "Ask yourself this question. Why is it dark only over North Light, and us?"

James glanced around. Eugene was right. The rest of the island, as far as he could see, shined in bright daylight. North Light, the beach surrounding it, and where they stood were swallowed in darkness.

"It's because we're in a time loop," Eugene said, as he took a few steps backward. "Well, I am at least. I thought Teagan could help me. As it turns out, you and I both need to find closure. I need to say goodbye to Amanda, and you need to realize by helping me it won't adversely affect anything in the future. My future is done. My future is finding peace. When you help me with that, then I will be able to move on."

Contemplating this for a moment, James understood what Eugene meant. He knew the old man was right. "Okay," he said. "I'll help." He stood up. Along with

Amanda and Teagan, he began the trek to the lighthouse.

Ester stayed behind saying, "It's kind of a long walk in the sand on the rocks for me. Even in my youth, I struggled with the hike. I'll wait for you here."

Eugene smiled broadly, and looked over at Ester. "Thank you. You've been a great friend." Eugene began what he hoped would be his last hike to North Light. In the dark, he heard a voice call out to him. Thinking it was James, he picked up the pace. He'd finally made it to the lighthouse path lined with beach plum plants on both sides. Eugene collapsed at the edge of the path within sight of the lighthouse. He felt a sharp twinge in his right arm. Lying on the sand for a few minutes, he attempted to gather his strength, without success.

Amanda walked up beside him. Touching his face, she felt stunned. "How?" is all she thought of to say. Forgetting the moment and the question, she bent over and helped her grandfather to his feet. Then with Eugene leaning against Amanda, the two of them made their way to the lighthouse. Eugene heard Amanda's breath as she held him close. Tears filled his eyes. "Amanda... your breathing... it's better." Amanda squeezed his side. "I'm glad you noticed. You don't have to worry about me anymore, Pop-Pop."

Eugene flopped down on the bench facing the flagpole. A tear falling from his eye, he turned to look at his granddaughter. "Amanda," he said. "North Light has always been my favorite place on Block Island. It's time to say goodbye."

Eugene reached out and hugged her so fiercely, he almost felt afraid that he'd crush her. He took one final look at his granddaughter and smiled. "I love you, Amanda." And then he rose from the bench and headed toward his final magnetic North. With his arms stretched out toward the lighthouse, as if to embrace it, a burst of white light enveloped the building. A loud noise that sounded like a sonic boom vibrated through the property. When the flash of light dissipated, Amanda saw what was left of her grandfather: small specks of exploding light floating skyward. She heard his voice one final time.

"I'll be back," he said. "And we'll always be together."

All became silent then and darkness turned to daylight. Amanda sat on the bench, weeping. As she looked up the path to the lighthouse, she thought about the day she'd had her first asthma attack. It was right here with her grandfather. They were racing along the path to the lighthouse. It was hot and the bushes around her smelled perfumed. All of a sudden, it felt like the air was thick and everything around her made it so she couldn't breathe. To make it seem less scary for her, her grandfather had given her a piggyback ride all the way back to the car.

A somber smile came to her face at the vivid memory. Even when she felt horrible, memories of her grandfather made her smile. After she had some time to grieve on her own, James and Teagan sat down beside her. They each took one of her hands.

James sat in the same spot Eugene had occupied moments before. Shaking his head in disbelief, he said, "Eugene was right." Looking into Amanda's eyes, he said, "I'm sorry. But I feel your grandfather has peace now. I hope you can find *your* peace."

James stood and helped Amanda to her feet. The three of them slowly walked back to the parking lot.

"This will always be my favorite place on the island," Amanda said, looking back at North Light. Her face was stained with tears, but she was smiling.

Together

Rylee Murphy wrapped Alex in a bear hug as the Block Island ferry docked at the Old Harbor Landing. She adjusted her backpack and smiled wide, so much so it almost hurt. Releasing from the embrace, she said, "You're gonna love it here, Alex. My uncle used to bring me to the island when I was young, and I fell in love with this place."

"I can't wait, Anima Mia."

She twisted a lock of blond hair between her fingers and took his hand as they disembarked. Blushing at the name Alex had given her, Rylee couldn't help but feel special. Seagulls squawked overhead, looking for handouts. The sun created flashes of light in the water, making it sparkle. Rylee pushed through the crowd. "We gotta go to Finn's. They have the best food on the island. But first, we should head to Wendy's.

Over the years, Rylee had cultivated several close friends who lived on the island. These friendships came with guest rooms versus the inordinately expensive hotel and inn prices when the tourist season was at full peak. Wendy happened to be one such friend. Gone for a week visiting her own family on the mainland, she told Rylee that she could stay at her place for the weekend. Bikes, and Wendy's own car, were available for use as well. They walked up through the parking lot and stopped at one of the taxi stands. A van with "Monica's Taxi" emblazoned on the passenger door stood idling. "Can you bring us to 620 Corn Neck Road? We're staying there for the weekend."

"That's Wendy Parker's place," the taxi driver said.

"Yes indeed," Rylee smiled. "Wendy and I have been friends for years. She's off island visiting her family this week and told me I could have free reign of the place for the weekend."

"Hop in," the taxi driver said. "I'm Monica, by the way."

Alex went around back and tossed their overnight bags in, then returned to the front of the van, and opened the door for Rylee. After she was seated, he climbed in and they were off.

Rylee and Alex had been friends for over five years. Best friends. They met in a bookstore while attending an event about gravestone etchings. Alex felt an instant connection and asked her if she wanted to grab a coffee. After she agreed, their friendship began. That instant connection rarely happened to him. Even his previous relationship took time to develop, but this was something different. The feeling caught him entirely off guard. Not simply physical; although, he couldn't deny her looks attracted him. That long blond hair and her blue eyes certainly moved him to forget his trepidation. Her smile, the final nail impressed upon him the need to take the chance. The phrase soulmate ran through his head. Alex shook it away with the inner reasoning that he'd just finished reading a manuscript about past lives. Yet that first time together after the bookstore event continued to haunt him. He couldn't shake the feeling that there was something special about this young woman. Alex had the innate feeling that she felt the same.

Neither were dating at the time. Alex's last relationship ended the year before. He thought everything had been going well, until one morning his girlfriend decided differently. Heartbroken, Alex retreated from everyone. Work and home became his world. He worked as an editor with a publisher in Connecticut. The biggest perk of his position was the ability to work from home, or anywhere else for that matter. He escaped into his work, so as not to think about his breakup. When he heard about the gravestone etching event at the local bookstore, he decided to venture out.

Being a book editor provided him an excuse for attending. It was really the first time since his breakup that he made the decision to go out. All this time later, Alex wondered what would have happened if he hadn't gone to the bookstore program that night. Would their paths have crossed at some other point? His thoughts returned to the soulmate idea. Did he believe that? He'd always been fascinated by the subject, a natural progression from gravestone etching, he liked to think.

Rylee had been in one long-term relationship. Unlike Alex, Rylee's relationship ended amicably for both parties. They realized after two years that they both wanted different things. No drama. No heartbreak. The relationship simply ran its course, and both were okay with its dissolution.

Since Alex and Rylee had been friends, they dated other people, but nothing really took hold. Neither were jealous of the other. Though as time passed and they spent more of that time together, Alex began developing deeper feelings for Rylee. He wanted more. He understood Rylee's caution. She didn't want to lose their friendship. Willing to take the chance for something more meaningful, Alex pressed her a few times to reconsider. When he realized he ran the risk of losing everything, he pulled back. Through dating others, late-night phone calls, and texting at all hours of the day and night, finding time to stay together was paramount to them. Rylee couldn't see her life without Alex in it and she felt fearful that if they did move forward and something happened, they'd both be devastated. No pressure involved. Never any fear of breaking up and losing each other. That's what motivated Rylee not to get more involved.

Although she couldn't deny the attraction to Alex. His dark complexion and jet-black hair, his five-foot eight-inch frame, a complete opposite to her own blond hair and five-foot-four became a running-opposites attraction trope. It wasn't just his looks that drew Rylee in. His politeness wasn't simply a game he played. It wasn't something he did at the beginning of the friendship to cement the relationship. To this day, five years in, Alex continued to do things that most couples wouldn't. He still held doors for her before he went through. He still pulled her chair out first when they sat down to eat. He still surprised her by cooking her favorite meal on occasion, grilled tuna steak, broccoli and mashed potatoes. So many other things he did too. No wonder people who saw them together thought they were married or at least dating.

"Here we are," Monica said, pulling up to the front of 620 Corn Neck Road.

Alex looked out the side window and saw a great blue heron swoop down over the property, its wings out and finally coming in for a landing in the water, just out of earshot. He saw the bird hit the water with precision. "Beautiful spot," he said stepping out of the taxi and retrieving their overnight bags from the back of the van. "There's water everywhere. I can't believe your friend is just letting us stay here."

"You ain't seen nothing yet," Rylee said, sticking her head out the passenger window. Then looking at Monica, she said, "How do you know Wendy?" Rylee looked out the front windshield, the ocean directly in front of her. "This is why I love it here. So many people rave about Martha's Vineyard. For someone who needs the water, Block Island is the only place to visit.

Monica glanced at Rylee. "A small island such as this, it isn't hard to know the islanders who have lived here most of their lives. Wendy grew up here. Her family owned this house before her. We met, I don't know," Monica closed her eyes, attempting to extract the piece of information, "maybe six years ago. She needed a ride home because a date she went on turned sideways. She found my taxi outside the Mohegan Café and we've been friends ever since. How do you know her?"

"At first," Rylee said, "she was a client. My sister, Teagan and I have a design firm. We mostly concentrate on artists, photographers, writers and painters."

"Oh, yeah," Monica said. "I've seen her artwork. She is quite adept.

"I saw Wendy's artwork hanging in a gallery on the mainland. I loved how she captured Block Island in watercolor and oils. Many artists only excel in one medium, but Wendy managed to master two. Thanks for the lift. What do we owe?"

"Seven-fifty," Monica said.

Rylee pulled her pack off and reached in to grab her wallet. "Here's a ten," she said. "Keep the change."

"Thanks. Enjoy the weekend," Monica said and drove off.

Rylee dug around in her backpack for the house key that Wendy mailed to her the week before. She found it in zipped up pocket inside the bag. When she walked inside, she saw a piece of paper on the counter.

Hi Rylee:

So sorry we couldn't see each other this time. Enjoy your weekend. And remember, mi casa su casa. I can't wait to meet Alex. Next time. I left the AC running when I went off island. I know how much you like your cold. Hope Alex doesn't freeze. But then... LOL

Luv ya,

Wendy

P.S. By the way, the car's all gassed up and there are bikes in the shed.

Alex easily pictured himself living here. Wide hardwood floors. Floor to ceiling windows throughout, letting in maximum light during the summer. A sofa, a rocking chair with a quilted Red Sox blanket hanging over the back, and a coffee table sat in the middle of the living room. A dining room table sat off to the left near the kitchen. Two large windows in front of the dining table looked out at the water in the backyard. "This place is magnificent." Alex continued to look around.

Rylee walked up next to him. "There's a bedroom here on the first floor. And three more upstairs. They all have queen-sized beds with their own bathrooms."

"I don't care. Where do you want to sleep?" Alex asked. In the five years they'd been friends and spent time together overnight, neither one had ever considered sleeping together. It wasn't on their radar. However, with everything that happened now, they were both thinking the same thing but were afraid to discuss it. "I'll stay down here," Alex said. He quickly unloaded his belongings from his bag and brought the other bag upstairs for Rylee.

"You didn't have to do that."

He smiled. "That's alright. Shall we head back downtown?"

"Sure, let's bike," Rylee said, thinking about the surprise she had planned for Alex. Biking would be quicker. Fifteen to twenty minutes as opposed to almost an hour to get where she wanted to bring him for the surprise.

They went to the shed and found two bikes. Rylee hopped on hers and Alex grabbed his. "First up, is Finn's Seafood," Rylee said, pulling onto Corn Neck Road. "I like their veggie tacos best, plus my friend, Gary Mott manages the place."

They turned onto Dodge Street, passing the Blue Dory Inn then the Island library, and this made Rylee think about her Uncle Chris. She remembered countless times when he talked about moving here and getting a job at the library. He never did. They turned the corner and went by the National Hotel. They made their way to Finn's outside window on the deck, he scanned the menu attached to the wall. "Do you feel like a veggie taco or fried artichoke hearts?" he asked, pointing to the menu.

"Sticking with the veggie taco." Rylee pointed to a table at the back of the deck. "How about we sit over there?" she said, strolling over to the empty table. She took off her backpack and placed it on the chair beside her.

Alex wiped a bead of sweat from his brow. "You're probably right about the veggie tacos. Sounds good to me. Go sit down, Anima Mia, and I'll order our food."

Rylee felt that tinge of embarrassment again. Smiling, an electric charge surged through her as always when Alex used that pet name. It was almost the same feeling as when her feet touched Block Island every year. Hearing Alex use that term of endearment meant more to her once she realized that it meant "my soul" in Italian. It sometimes embarrassed her, however, especially when they were in public. It always led to the inevitable question of why they weren't together. With such a passionate turn of phrase, it's obvious why people would interpret their actions as being romantic. Turning her attention from her inner thoughts, Rylee adjusted her chair, so she faced the sidewalk outside the porch. She loved people-watching, here on Block Island in particular.

211 C. Jennings Penders

As she turned back to see Alex at the window, she thought again how fortunate she was to have found such a good man to be friends with. The movie *When Harry Met Sally* always floated through her periphery when she thought about him. She couldn't keep her reflections from returning to their friendship for long. During their five years together, Rylee often thought about what it would be like if they moved their relationship to a new level. They'd even discussed it, several times. Rylee worried if they move forward and something went wrong, then all would be lost in their best interest. She loved Alex more than anything and couldn't bear the thought of not being in his life. However, there was nothing romantic in that love. That's what she told herself at least. She felt safe with him and always had.

Once at the window, a waitress popped out. "What can I get you and your wife?" she asked, glancing at Rylee

Alex smiled. "Two veggie taco platters, please. And a grilled artichoke, please."

The waitress reached under the window and handed Alex a painted stone with the numeral 4 on it. "Good choice. We'll call your number when the food is ready. Please bring this stone back to get your tray. Enjoy Block Island.

Seagulls squawked and continued to swoop around other tables nearby, hoping someone would be generous enough to either purposely give scraps, or accidentally drop something.

The speakers at the restaurant came to life. "Number four and number six. Your trays are ready. Please remember to return your stones."

Alex got up and walked back to the window. He returned the stone and picked up the tray with two lobster sandwiches, French fries, and two small coleslaws.

He carried the tray back to the table, maneuvering around others as they walked up to order. The middle of July always had an influx of tourists, both a boon and a curse. Weekdays were less crowded than weekends. Fortunately, Rylee and Alex had the flexibility to take time off from work at their discretion. With Alex being a book editor, he could delegate. Rylee sometimes helped Alex read and comment on the slush pile that came through. She'd even found a few promising manuscripts that were now going through further review. She'd been a voracious reader, even as a young girl. This was something else she attributed to her uncle who'd been a librarian his entire life. When Rylee wasn't reading from the slush pile, she worked with her sister Teagan at Tealee Design.

As he began to eat his taco, a section broke off and fell out onto the pavement. In that moment, one of the seagulls swooped down, scurried under the table, picked up the lobster, and flew away with a squawk. It almost seemed like a celebration.

Rylee laughed out loud. "See? These birds know what they're doing."

Even though it meant losing a piece of his food, Alex couldn't help but laugh too. Smiling at Rylee, he said, "You love it here, don't you?"

Rylee swept that lock of hair away from her face again. "I hope you come to love this island like I do. There's really nowhere else I'd rather be and no one else I'd rather be here with."

Alex smiled as they finished eating. When done, he returned the trays while Rylee went to their bikes and waited for Alex. When he joined her, taking hold of his bicycle, Rylee said, "I have a surprise for you."

They biked passed Ballard's then turned onto Chapel Street., then left onto Old Town Road. Biking by Club Soda, Rylee said, "I've never eaten there, but I know people say it's good." From Old Town Road, they turned onto Center Road.

So, you gonna tell me where we are going?"

Rylee was a few feet in front. She looked back. "It wouldn't be a surprise if I told you, now would it?" As they continued, the sun went behind the clouds, providing some cooling relief for a moment. There were many people out walking, biking, and riding mopeds.

Alex caught up with her. "I can't imagine what this place will be tomorrow. I bet Saturdays in the summer are outrageous."

"Yeah," Rylee took one hand off the handlebars and rubbed her eye. "Friday nights are crazy downtown too. You're right, though. Saturdays are insane. Tourists coming and going. It's probably the busiest time of the season. We're almost there." As she said that, they stopped at Island Cemetery. Rylee reached into her pack and pulled out two etching pads and two charcoal pencils. Giving one to Alex, she said, "Knock yourself out!"

Now it was his turn to give Rylee a bear hug. "Oh my, Anima Mia!" Goose bumps rose on his arms. He laughed out loud and ran into the cemetery, carrying the etching pad in one hand and the charcoal pencil in the other. He almost floated on air. Rylee loved to surprise him like this. It was the first time in a while that she saw Alex so excited. It warmed her heart to still delight him when she could. This trip to Block Island was a surprise for him, and bringing him to this cemetery was as much of a delight for him as it was for her. She strolled through, taking time to study gravestones. They ended up stopping together at the same family plot. The gravestone read "Alan and Mary Littlefield, husband and wife."

Alex felt dumbfounded when he saw the birthdate for Alan. December twelfth was his birthday as well! "Do you see this, Rylee?" He pointed to Alan's birthdate on the stone. He opened the etching pad and placed a piece of paper against the stone. About to start a rubbing, a spark of energy ran through his hand. "What the..." His vision clouded. For a brief moment, he found himself in a small room with wood paneled walls and a single bed. He saw an old man lying in the bed. The old man raised his head, and he said in a distressed voice, "What's happening, Anima Mia? I love you, Mary. I'm not ready to leave you yet." Just as suddenly, he was back at the present-day cemetery.

Alex stumbled back, his mouth agape. "What the… what was that? Did you hear that, Rylee?"

"Hear what?" She went to help him up. "Are you alright?" She steadied him on his feet. She could tell he was unsure of his footing. He fell back, reaching out for one of the headstones to keep him from falling completely to the ground. "I don't think you're okay to bike back to town, Alex. I'm going to call a taxi. Just sit here and rest a moment."

As he sat down and looked up at her. "Are you telling me you didn't see or hear anything?" He still couldn't put into words exactly what he thought had happened, and he wasn't sure he wanted to. Hearing someone else use his pet name for someone else really knocked him for a loop. Taken together with the fact that Alan's birthday as printed on the headstone was the same day as his spooked him beyond words. Could he even express this to Rylee? The whole thing sounded preposterous just thinking about it. How would it sound actually saying it out loud? He didn't quite understand what happened himself. How could he explain it to Rylee? Only one meaning made any sense, but Alex couldn't go there.

Rylee stayed right beside him while she called Monica's Taxi. Ten minutes later, Monica pulled up outside the cemetery. "Why hello again, you two," Monica said, when she pulled alongside the cemetery. "Where am I taking you?"

After Rylee helped Alex to his feet again, they slowly walked to the minivan. When they were buckled in the backseat, Rylee turned to him. "Maybe we should head back to Wendy's." Then she looked over at Alex. So, what exactly happened?" she asked

Alex looked out the window during the taxi ride. Taking a deep breath, he took Rylee's hand and squeezed it. "Something crazy!" It was all he said. As hard as he tried, he simply couldn't bring himself to tell her what he saw and heard. He was afraid that talking about it would make what happened real. Alex wasn't sure if what he experienced in the cemetery had even happened, or if it was simply a hallucination. How could he have heard someone use that same name; a name so uncommon he thought it impossible anyone else would know it? Anima Mia was their code word. Again, just one explanation seemed to make any kind of sense. Maybe on some level deep down, Alex hoped the explanation that he couldn't shake turned out to be the correct one. That he wasn't imagining things.

The taxi arrived at Wendy's for the second time that day. "Here we are," Monica said, as she pulled into a parking space. "That will be ten dollars, again," she said smiling."

Alex paid her, grabbed the bikes that Rylee put in the back and said, "Thank you." When they exited the cab and Monica pulled away, he looked over at Rylee. "I heard something at the cemetery," he said "And I saw something that defies reason."

They walked up to the porch and Rylee dug in her purse for the house keys. "Let's grab the car and head back downtown. Get some dinner? You can tell me what you experienced over a few glasses of wine."

"Sure," Alex said.

Rylee grabbed the car keys on the hook just inside. With keys in hand, they hopped in the Ford Escape that Wendy left for their use. Once downtown and parked, they decided to eat at the National. "Maybe we can get Bruce to come out and say hello," Rylee said. My uncle and he graduated high school together."

The hostess seated them at the end of the porch, closest to the Surf and overlooking the signature ninety-degree turn in the road.

A few minutes later, a waitress walked over with menus. "Can I offer you anything to drink while you look over the menu?"

"I'm going to skip the wine," Alex said, and ordered a glass of water with lemon. Rylee did the same.

When the waitress left, Alex brushed a hand through his course black hair. Taking a breath, he said, "I heard this old man call someone Anima Mia when I touched the gravestone. Then he called her Mary. He said he wasn't ready to leave her yet. That he loved her. That's *my* endearing name for you, Rylee. That's *ours*. And that cemetery plot was for Alan and Mary Littlefield, husband and wife. Did you see Alan's birthdate on his gravestone? Alan was born the same day as me!" Alex felt as though he was rambling. His voice trailed off after that. He turned away from Rylee, watching people, bikes, and mopeds fight for space on the street below the high dining porch.

In the time he spoke, their waitress returned with their waters.

Rylee sipped from hers. She put the glass down then smiled at the waitress. "Is Bruce here tonight?"

Their waitress nodded. "You know Bruce?"

"Yeah. My uncle and he were in the same high school class. Tell him Rylee Murphy is here."

"Have you decided what you want?"

Rylee ordered her favorite: grilled tuna steak, broccoli, and mashed potatoes. Alex went with wild salmon and asparagus.

After their waitress had gone, Rylee turned back to Alex. "You're wearing me down." She sighed here and looked out at the view. The seven o'clock evening ferry back to the mainland sat in the harbor with a line of people waiting to board. Cars waited in another line. Directly below the National, people jammed the sidewalks all along Water Street, entering and leaving the various storefronts. "What if we really are meant to be together?" Rylee said, feeling a chill go through her as she released those words. She noticed goose bumps rise over her arms. "Look at my arms," she said.

At the same moment, Alex felt goosebumps forming on his own arms as well. "It's what I've been trying to impress on you all these years. And if you believe what happened at the cemetery really happened, then even a grave can't separate us."

Their dinners arrived, giving Rylee a pause in the conversation and a moment to think about how she would respond. On the one hand, people did think they were together. Wherever they went, they were constantly thought of as husband and wife. Maybe it was time to move forward and make that commitment of intimacy, and take the risk. But then she considered the other side; she couldn't bear losing him as a friend. A silent voice inside became almost deafening in her head. How much longer do you think he will wait? What happens when he meets someone who does want something more? She shook the voice away and picked up her fork. Ignoring the conversation, she began to eat.

Silence being the only thing on the menu as they ate, they did their best to avoid the bull in the china shop.

After Alex took his last bite, he smiled at Rylee. "You know I love you, Anima Mia." It was the first time he called her that since the cemetery. "And I certainly don't want to lose this, he said, indicating with his hands the relationship they developed. "But don't you think we deserve better?"

Rylee blushed, turning beet red. "I love you, too Alex. You know that."

"I know you do." He drew in a breath and considered his next words carefully, but then decided to simply say what he wanted and to hell with the consequences. "What if what happened today is another sign that we are supposed to be together? Romantically, I mean."

Rylee pushed that same strand of hair away from her face. "Another sign?" "Oh my gosh. Are you kidding me?" Alex took the last sip from his water, placed the glass back on the table, and let out a deep breath. "We should be together."

"Of course, I've thought about it. But we've been through this countless times. Do you really want to talk about it again?" Rylee sat back in her chair and stretched her legs out. "You know how I feel about this."

Rylee was saved from the conversation when she heard her name called from somewhere down the long porch. She turned to see Bruce Pigott approaching. "When Tina told me you were here, I had to come out and say hello. Are you here long?"

"Just for the weekend." She turned to Alex. "Bruce, this my friend, Alex."

Bruce reached out and they shook hands. "Nice to meet you. Don't let this one go, Alex. She's pretty amazing."

"Ahhhh. Don't encourage him, Bruce." She laughed.

"Have you seen Sean yet?"

"We're planning on stopping by the Spring House sometime tomorrow," Rylee said.

"Tell him I said hello and I expect to see him soon. And by the way, don't even consider paying for your dinners tonight."

"Oh no, Bruce. We can't let you do that."

"Rylee," he said, giving her the look that said don't argue.

Sighing, she relented. "Thanks."

"Okay. Well. I gotta get back to work. I'm so happy I got to see you. And nice meeting you Alex. I hope I get to see you again and remember what I said. Don't let Rylee slip away."

After Bruce left, Rylee and Alex made their way down the stairs to the street below. When they reached the sidewalk, Rylee guided Alex to the left. "I feel like some ice cream. There's a shop just up the street here." She passed a sign for a business she hadn't noticed earlier: Into the Past: Brian Weiss Trained Sessions/9 a.m. to 9 p.m. Daily/Appointments Preferred.

People in the spiritual world, those who studied past lives and reincarnation, all knew the name Brian Weiss. He rose to prominence in the late 1980s with the book, *Many Lives, Many Masters*. The book discussed a patient Weiss treated. Under deep hypnosis, this woman revealed stories of past lives she experienced. Weiss became well known after that and began training others in past life regression.

An arrow pointing down the same alley as the ice cream shop directed customers. "Okay. This is serendipitous," she said, pointing out the sign to Alex. "Let's stop in before we get our ice cream." She glanced at her watch. "It's not quite seven yet. There must be time to see if there are appointments for tomorrow."

Alex followed her inside with some trepidation. "I don't know. Do you really want to go down this path?"

Rylee opened the shop door, and a bell rang. With no hesitation, she said, "Darn straight, I do."

A woman's voice echoed from another room. "Be right there. Have a seat."

Rylee and Alex looked around the office. Pictures of a young woman and Brian Weiss hung throughout. A few minutes later, the same woman in the pictures arrived through a side door. She greeted the couple with her hand extended. "I'm Michelle Joy. I assume you're here to see *where* you were and *who* you were close to you in a previous life?"

In her mid-thirties, Michelle had an air of someone older and wiser, as if she herself was a very old soul, having lived many lifetimes on earth. Her hazel eyes expressed a knowledge beyond her years. Her light brown hair with a few streaks of grey lent an air of authenticity to the mature knowledge she seemed to exude. People who believed in past lives — and worked by helping others bridge the gap — were indeed old souls. She walked with purpose, and her strides impressed on Rylee that she took care of herself not just spiritually, but physically.

"I'm Rylee and this is Alex."

Michelle motioned to the sofa. "Please sit."

Rylee and Alex sat close. She turned to look him in the eye. He sighed. Nodding, he gave permission for her to go on.

"We came to Block Island this morning," Rylee said, and unconsciously reached for Alex's hand. "For the weekend. When we were touring around the island this afternoon, when we stopped at the Island Cemetery, you know, on the corner of West Side and Center Roads, and Alex had a rather strange occurrence."

Realizing he lost the battle to prevent any of this, Alex jumped in. "I came across a couple of stones in a family plot. Alan and Mary Littlefield. Alan was born on December 12. The same day as my own birthday. That in itself is kinda weird, but what happened next really freaked me out." He let out a long breath. Now fully engrossed in the story, Alex lost all concern he had felt when first entering the shop. "I placed a piece of paper to the stone, to do a gravestone rubbing, and that's when things went sideways."

Rylee watched Michelle and saw that she sat on the edge of her chair, clearly captivated.

"First I heard someone use a pet name that I use for Rylee. An unusual name, one so uncommon that I've never heard anyone else ever use it." He was smart enough to not mention the name. "And before you ask.

No, we are not currently, nor have Rylee and I ever dated each other. We're best friends only. But... Rylee seems convinced we need to figure out what my experience in the cemetery means. Have we been together before, in a past life? Do we need to reevaluate our current relationship? What if we are or *were* Alan and Mary Littlefield? I've done some reading on this subject. From what I've seen, they say that sometimes people who have been a couple in previous lives choose to be just friends in another life."

"That has happened," Michelle said, glancing at her watch. "In fact, just last month I counseled a couple in your same situation. Turned out they were married during their last two incarnations. Once I brought them to the place where we choose our life events just before we incarnate, the two of them simultaneously decided they wanted to be close friends in this, their current incarnation. No romantic attachment. They said they were given the choice to think about the decision. Ultimately, they went with just the friendship. For they knew they would always be together as friends or lovers. They wanted to see how living separately would change them, if at all."

Rylee looked over at Alex and smiled. A smile so deeply emotional, even Michelle reacted to the energy it exuded.

"You are definitely connected by something," Michelle said. "Deeper even than that last couple I mentioned." She looked down at her watch again.

"Holy..." She left the last word unsaid. "It's almost eight. I can't believe an hour has gone by. Can you come back tomorrow, say around ten o'clock? I believe there's something going on with the two of you. And just so you know, the way you act together. I hope I don't offend, but seeing you together, I'd have bet you were in a romantic relationship. You sit together close enough to be physical. You hold hands." She nodded to Rylee's intertwined hand with Alex. "And Alex? You told me you have a pet name for Rylee, an unusual name at that. Maybe on some level you both want to get closer. Do you date outside this friendship?"

They nodded.

"I bet nothing has gone beyond the second or third date with those other people."

Then they looked at each other.

"But Alex and I are just friends."

"There's no need to be embarrassed," Michelle said, standing up. "Sometimes it takes another person to point out the obvious. As the saying goes, 'You can't see the forest for the trees.' Although, it could be you're both having residual feelings from a past life. Block Island seems to do that, attract magic and the etheric. It's what drew *me* to this island, to live, and why I opened this business. Okay," she said, heading for the door, "now I really have to go. See you tomorrow ten o'clock."

They all exited the shop together. Michelle locked the door and headed off down the walkway between buildings, while Rylee and Alex went to their car, having forgotten about their original intention to get ice cream.

Both were lost in thought as they passed the now dark and silent ocean. The ocean was just like them, dark and silent, but moving just below the surface was something wild, turbulent, and energetic. A buzzing surrounded them; something only they felt. No words needed to be spoken. No words ever needed to be said between them. They were connected by something beyond love, beyond friendship. If nothing else came of the meeting the next morning, the two of them at least understood that now.

When they arrived at Wendy's, they were exhausted from the day. Before heading to bed, Alex said, "Hope you sleep well. I saw a place right where the ferry docked today that we can go for breakfast before meeting Michelle tomorrow. And it's right downtown. Ernie's?"

"I love Ernie's," Rylee said. "Yeah. Let's do that." She walked to the bedroom. "Good night, Alex." She heard him descend the stairs, then close his bedroom door.

As she lay in bed, Rylee couldn't help but think what may have happened if Alex hadn't volunteered to sleep downstairs. Neither one of them was really ready to be sleeping in the same room together, but the events over the past day had certainly left an impression of a much greater closeness between them than either would accept. During the last five years together—where so many people thought they were romantically tied—and this trip to Block Island seemed to push them closer than ever.

Rylee lay in bed and went over the day's events. She wondered, not for the first time, if she was unconsciously sabotaging her dates with other men because she truly only wanted that one man who was just down the stairs below her. She tried to shake the feeling, but it wouldn't relent. With Alex just downstairs from her, she felt more alone tonight than at any other time she and Alex were in close proximity. She tried to shake that feeling as well. Rolling over on her left side, she pulled the covers up and closed her eyes, thinking dichotomous thoughts. She fell asleep hearing Michelle saying, "I bet your dates don't go much beyond two or three."

She slept fitfully through the night, waking up the next morning when she heard Alex in the kitchen running water from the faucet. She glanced at the clock beside the bed. The glowing red numbers showed 6:45.

Rylee threw the covers off and stumbled into the bathroom, rubbing her eyes, still half asleep. "Hopefully a shower will wake me up," she said out loud to herself. She threw some cold water on her face before showering.

She walked downstairs and saw Alex sitting at the dining table deep in thought, looking out the window at the water. Rylee wondered if he had the same thoughts swimming through his head—that perhaps they really were supposed to be together.

"Good Morning!" she said, with more cheer than she felt. "Shall we get ready and head to town for that breakfast you thought about last night?"

He didn't answer, still looking out the window, still deep in thought.

"Alex?" Rylee walked over to him and touched his shoulder.

He jumped out of his chair. Laughing and trying to catch his breath, he said, "Wow! Have you been here long?"

Now Rylee knew he was thinking the same thing. It's one of the features of any long-term friendship, the ability to know what the other person is thinking. And the talent to complete each other's sentences, which they did all the time. "No. I was just asking if you wanted to head to Ernie's for breakfast."

Getting up and pushing the chair back closer to the table, he asked, "Sure. How did you sleep?"

"I always miss my own bed. I've slept here before, so it's not so bad." Rylee headed for the door. Looking back, she said, "I don't know about you but I need my iced coffee."

He smiled. "Okay. Let's get our breakfast. And you your coffee."

When they arrived in town, even though it wasn't eight o'clock yet, there were already cars parked everywhere.

"People like to get a head start here, don't they?" Alex said.

Rylee glanced out the driver's side window. "She drove past the National and found a space close to where they had parked the night before. They were seated at Ernie's a few minutes later, after the long walk to the south end of Water Street, where Ernie's was located, near the rotary sporting Rebecca at the Well in the center, that white-stone statue in flowing robe, holding a vase as if she were pouring water from it.

Rylee looked at the Rebecca statue for a moment, before entering the restaurant. She had long known the statue as there—an old water fountain installed at the end of the 19th century, someone had told her, and that it had ceased working long ago—but she had never really considered the statue. Thinking back to the meeting with Michelle last night, and her thoughts of past lives, she could not help but imagine the statue as a living person for a moment. When she entered Ernie's as Alex held the door, she was very happy that Alex was a flesh and blood man, and she felt a tingle deep in her chest when she felt his physical warmth as she passed close in front of him.

Once served, Rylee immediately took one long sip of her iced coffee and sighed. "Now I'm feeling better."

Their waiter returned to take their order. Rylee ordered a stack of pancakes, hash browns, and bacon.

"So predictable," Alex said, grinning. "I could have ordered for you. I'll have two Belgium waffles, turkey sausage, and an orange juice. Large." The waiter reached across the table and took Rylee's menu and handed both back to the waiter. "I'm having an amazing time here, Rylee. Yesterday kinda freaked me out, but I'm glad you're here with me."

After their food arrived, Rylee reached for the ketchup. "We'll figure this out," she said as she spread ketchup on her hash browns. That was something Alex could never understand, ketchup on hash browns. Rylee dug her fork in to the hash browns. "Mmm. So delicious," she said and smiled. Alex laughed.

When they finished, they decided to stroll along Water Street, looking at the shops, before their appointment with Michelle on the other side of the downtown.

"I want to bring you to North Light later," Rylee said. "My uncle loved it there, and now it's become my favorite place on the island. Something about it has always fascinated me, and it isn't just that my uncle loved it. There's something more. I can't quite put my finger on why."

They walked into Star Department Store and up the ramp. Rylee found a blue tee shirt for Alex. "Extra-large, right?"

He smiled.

She never did understand why he liked his shirts two sizes too big. But she did know that blue was his favorite color. She went to the register and cashed out.

"We'll come back and look around more later. We should get to our appointment."

While continuing on, Alex felt suddenly queasy. His stomach lurched and his heart began to beat a little faster. He rested his hand on his chest and felt his heart. Just nerves, he thought. "Maybe I shouldn't have had those waffles." He stopped in the middle of the sidewalk and took a breath.

"Are you alright?" She went back to him and waited until he gathered his strength.

"I'm fine. Just don't know what to expect. I'm still a little freaked out from yesterday." Alex took one more slow, deep breath in and let it out. "Okay. Let's move."

They arrived at Michelle's just a little after ten. Alex knocked and went in with Rylee following behind.

Michelle was waiting for them. "Right on time," she said. "I hope you slept well last night. I'm sure you're still dealing with some residual effects. Hopefully we can resolve the issues." She looked at Alex. "Since the event happened to you, we can start with you. I'd like you to come with us, Rylee." She guided them into another room. "Take a seat there, Alex." Michelle pointed to a recliner in the corner of the room. "Just relax. I can tell you're nervous."

Alex sat down, stretched his legs, and closed his eyes.

"Okay, Alex. Breath slowly. I'm going to put on some music for you. We'll be out in the next room." Michelle flipped her computer on and found some Enya to play. When the music started, she guided Rylee into the front room. "We'll give him about ten minutes, and then we'll go in again. While we're waiting, let's talk. How long have you and Alex been friends?"

"We met a little more than five years ago. We both attended a gravestone etching event run by a local bookstore."

"And what do you remember when meeting Alex for the first time?"

"I felt an instant connection when he walked into the bookstore. Then, all during the event, I couldn't stop looking over at him. After the event, he asked if I wanted to get coffee." Rylee couldn't control the smile emerging on her face when she recalled that day.

"I'm guessing you took him up on that coffee?"

"Yes. That connection I felt doesn't happen often, and I didn't want to let it pass. So, we had coffee and we've been friends ever since."

Michelle adjusted in her chair. "I'm going to be forward here. Has your friendship with Alex ever caused hiccups in your dating life?"

"That's another yes. We dated others throughout our friendship, and neither one of us felt threatened by any of the dates we'd been on. Although last night I started to wonder about something you said." Rylee looked up. "You said you bet the dates we went on with others didn't go beyond the second or third date."

"How many fourth dates have your or Alex had since becoming friends?"

"That would be zero. I wonder now if I wasn't self-sabotaging them because I wanted to be with Alex."

"Have you spoken with him about it since the cemetery?"

"Not really."

"We'll resolve this." Michelle got up. "Let's go check on Alex now."

They walked into the room and found him sitting in the chair, both feet on the seat, lotus style. Rylee saw the position he was in and smiled. Rylee whispered to Michelle. "That's how he sits when he's comfortable, when he's not worried about a thing."

"You know him quite well." Michelle sat down in the chair opposite him and gestured to Rylee to sit next to her in the other chair. "Alex?"

He nodded

"Do you know where you are?"

"On Block Island."

"Good. Now I want you to start counting back from one hundred. When you reach sixty, you'll open your eyes, but stay relaxed and continue counting slowly backward."

Alex agreed and in monotone he started, "100, 99, 98..."

Upon request, when he reached sixty, his eyes fluttered open. Michelle could see he was still in a state of relaxation, a state of bliss.

"Okay. We're going to take you on a little journey back to yesterday. Do you remember what happened?" Michelle waited while Alex thought back.

"We went to the Island Cemetery to do some gravestone etchings. I found a gravestone that had my birthday engraved on it." He stopped there and began to tremble. "Wait a minute," he said. "It was our plot."

Rylee looked over at Michelle and gasped. Michelle motioned to hush Rylee. "Let him continue."

"I placed my paper against my stone, and that's when I heard the voice and saw the vision. A room with an old man lying in a bed. He rose off his pillow and said 'I'm not ready to leave you yet, Anima Mia. I love you Mary.'"

"You said it was your plot. Whose plot do you mean?"

A chill rose through him and goose bumps rose all over his body. He slumped backward, his mouth opened, and his head went to the back of the chair. His eyelids fluttered as if he were in REM sleep.

"Are you still with us, Alex?"

"Yeeeesss." The single word was drawn out. His voice sounded far away as if it traveled through a pipeline. Alex continued to slump in his chair, and his eyelids continued to flutter.

"Where are you, Alex?"

"Somewhere…" He stopped. "…beautiful. So much light. Blinding. There's a hole in the sky. My God, Mary is here too. She's right by my side. Wait a minute…" He

235 C. Jennings Penders

gasped. "No! It's Rylee. We're all glowing. So blinding. I think we are going down. I reach out to hold your hand, but you fall away from me. Before I lose sight of you, I hear you say, 'I'll see you soon, Anima Mia.' Then you vanish. Your light flickers, then fades away completely. I momentarily feel disoriented without you. But that passes as I drift down and feel myself becoming heavier, growing flesh."

Rylee couldn't believe what she was hearing. The pieces began to fit together in a beautiful mosaic. She tried to speak, but no words came. All she could do was listen to her soul mate's vision. She was convinced now. "Oh my gosh! I called him Anima Mia first when we separated." Her mouth dropped open. "Of course. My soul. We are connected by our souls." Tears streamed down her face.

"Alright," Michelle said. "I'm going to bring you back. I will count to ten and with each number you will become more aware of your surroundings. One. Two. Three. Your eyes open."

Alex shuttered. His eyes flickered several times as if attempting to refocus. He gazed clearly, directly into Rylee's eyes.

"Four. Five. Six."

He moved his legs to the floor.

"Seven. Eight."

He attempted to speak but no words came.

"Nine. Ten. You are now fully back, and you remember everything from your experience here today."

"Oh my Gosh!" Alex exclaimed. "It's you, Anima Mia. It's always been you! It was our plot at the cemetery yesterday." Tears welled in his eyes. "I see that now. We are Alan and Mary Littlefield! We are supposed to be together. We've *always* been together." He leapt out of the chair and embraced her. "I love you, Rylee!" He couldn't stop trembling. He pulled away and caressed her face. "It's you, Rylee. It's you. It's always been you!"

Rylee hugged him closer. Each not wanting to let the other go. She swung one hand free, took his hand, intertwined her fingers into his, and kissed him gently on the lips.

It was their first physical touch other than holding hands. A jolt of electricity bounced between them. Sparks flew through the room. Two souls becoming one. They reluctantly pulled away from each other and sat down on the sofa but continued to lock eyes.

Michelle broke the connection. "That was amazing! As many times as I've seen these things play out, I'm never short of amazed. Not many people have the benefit to know beyond doubt that they chose this life and their romantic partners. That's why I do what I do. This feeling never gets old." She smiled. "Bringing two people closer and showing them that death is simply a transition, that what's left behind is never truly gone, makes my world brighter. It gives my clients peace knowing that they will always find each other."

On some level, Rylee knew all along that Alex was her soul mate. Like Alex, she'd been afraid to speak up because of fear. She had feared losing Alex if something went sideways. It took Alex coming to Block Island — and experience at the cemetery — to solidify the relationship. What if this trip hadn't happened? What if they hadn't gone to Island Cemetery?

What if?

What if?

They were together now and always would be. That's all that mattered.

Rylee stood up and Alex followed. "We can't thank you enough, Michelle. Without you, we would never have seen the present and the past come together, and show us what we were missing for the future." Rylee gave Michelle a hug then she and Alex stepped out into the bright sun of the island.

"What do you say, Alex? Should we take that drive to the North Light?"

End of Season

E ster sat at her kitchen table, dressed for the day and sipping her first cup of coffee, when a knock on the front door interrupted her most peaceful time of the day Who could be knocking at seven-forty-five in the morning? Opening the door, she found Tom Norris standing on her porch. He smiled. "Hi Ester." The sun had begun to warm the island, but it didn't get past 80 degrees since it was now early September. When a breeze blew, it started warm but left Ester with a chill. Autumn had begun to show its face.

"Don't kill the messenger," Tom said, brushing his long hair away from his face. "Bruce said to bring you to the National before you made breakfast."

Damn them, she thought. Ester knew what this was about. After all, it was September third. She looked away for a moment, shaking her head. No use in arguing. "So," Ester said, grabbing her house keys,

"When are you planning on getting that haircut? You're looking a little shaggy."

"You're not the first person to say so. But this look has been part of who I am for as long as I can recall. It isn't that easy to give up something you've been doing almost your entire life."

"Regardless, Tom, I think you'd look much more handsome with a haircut. Who knows? Maybe a young woman would be drawn to you as well."

He blushed a little. "I'll think about it."

"Good." She paused, then said, "So, there's breakfast waiting for me at the National and you know nothing about it?"

"Of course, I do. It's our annual end of season celebration. You know as well as all Islanders do that we do this every year the first week in September."

He's right, she thought. Maybe that's all this happened to be. Ester climbed into Tom's truck and her aging body creaked as she reached around to buckle in.

While driving toward town Tom quickly looked over at Ester. "We wanted to include you last year too," he said. "But you were off-island. Even though you're not a business owner, you've been a friend and more, to so many. We want to show you how much you mean to us."

Now she realized that's what this really was about, the annual wrap-up of the season. She felt foolish thinking it could've been anything else. Besides, only Teagan knew the other significance of September third.

And Ester trusted that Teagan wouldn't divulge the importance of the day unless Ester gave her permission.

As they turned on Dodge Street and parked behind the National, Ester adjusted herself in the cab facing Tom. "I'm glad you stopped by," she said. "And thank you for making sure I was a part of today's celebration."

Tom took Ester's arm in his and escorted her through the rear entry of the broad hotel lobby, and proceeded straight through to the front porch.

Seated at a large table half way down the porch were Sean from the Spring House and Sean's new romantic partner, Heather Littlefield, who was Bruce's sous chef. James and his new friend, Rebecca, who he'd been seeing all season, sat at the table as well. And of course, Amanda, and Teagan were there too.

These were the most important people in Ester's life. And they were all here on September third. Standing among her seated friends, she began to wonder if someone *did* know that today was of particular importance to Ester.

That's when more people started ambling in: Cheryl and Ed Ball, Jennifer Cartwright, Gary Mott, and Helen Johnson. They pulled more small tables together to make a second single large table.

"Are you sure all these people are hear just to celebrate the end of the summer season?" Ester said.

"I thought we already went through this," Tom said. "Is there some reason that today is significant for you?"

Silence reigned.

Helen asked, "What else could it be, Ester?

"Ask if it's her birthday!" Cheryl said a bit loud. "It's the only thing that makes sense."

She realized then that there'd be no denying it. So, sighing, Ester said, "Yes. September third is my birthday."

"Well now," Bruce said, appearing before the crowd. "We have another reason to celebrate together. Why keep it a secret?"

"I didn't plan on keeping my birthday from everyone. It's just that... I don't know... I guess I don't like a fuss being made over me."

"But you've done so much for everyone sitting here this morning," Bruce explained. "I think in one way or another, you've facilitated some of our friendships. Teagan and Amanda most recently. I think it's time we celebrate you, Ester."

Bruce guided her to Teagan's table. Then he walked into the hotel and returned a moment later with helpers carrying trays of food, along with a cake with one candle burning in the center. "Kind of early in the day for a cake," Bruce said, "but we wanted to celebrate right away." Bruce grabbed a seat next to Amanda and everyone began grabbing food from the trays.

A gentle breeze floated through the porch, blowing a few napkins off the tables.

Utensils scraped against plates and coffee mugs hit the tables and everyone ate joyously. There was some small talk among those gathered, but mostly everyone enjoyed the food that Bruce and Heather had prepared early that morning. Jennifer broke the silence of everyone eating.

"I know we've never officially met, Ester. But I feel like I know you from what all these people have told me, and I hope to spend some time with you in the coming year. I'm Jennifer Cartwright. Eric Thomas and I are the couple from the Ocean View Hotel. The couple who realized they were in the fire that burned the hotel to the ground back in 1966," she said. "We're learning so much about each other now, and I wish Michelle Joy, with her amazing psychic talents, was able to join us this morning. She's given us so much insight into our lives, both present and past."

"Michelle wished she could have been here this year too," Bruce interjected. "Her business brought her off island last night, however. You can probably catch up with her next week, Jennifer. I'm sure she'd love to hear your story."

Amanda smiled at Ester. "Were it not for you," she said, "I wouldn't have had the chance to say goodbye to my grandfather. I'll say it again. You have no idea how many people you've influenced here." Amanda gestured at the tables. "This is just a sampling. Happy birthday, Ester."

She found this attention disconcerting. While Ester enjoyed the presence of one or two friends showering her with love, all these people at once felt like overkill.

243 C. Jennings Penders

She understood that her friends wanted to express their gratitude. "This is way too much," Ester said, smiling. "You folks are amazing. And all this fuss. It's why I wanted to keep my birthdate a secret. But I do love all of you, and thank you so much!" She moved closer to Teagan and whispered into her ear. "Did you tell anyone what today is?"

Shaking her head, no, Teagan reached out and hugged Ester. "You've been more than a grandmother to me." Choking up, she said, "You've been a confidant. You've been my friend. You've been a pain in the ass." She laughed out loud. "But you push me to do things I wouldn't do otherwise. You have pointed me in the direction of something I already knew and didn't want to hear. Something I needed to do that I didn't want to do. You are an amazing person. Happy birthday, Ester."

The crowd followed suit, saying in unison: "Happy birthday, Ester!"

After everyone returned to eating, Bruce said to the group, "Now let's talk about this season. I understand it's only start of September and you still have to verify your accounting, but some of you *must* have an inkling of how well you did this season."

"Thanks to Sean," Tom said, "I've been able to take some time away from the Spring House. I trust him implicitly. And I think I've finally broken down his resistance."

"You mean broken him in, Tom?" someone said.

"Yeah," Tom said, sweeping a large swath of hair away from his eyes.

"You wouldn't have to keep doing that if you finally gave up that mane of yours and went to the barber."

"Who said that?" Tom wanted to know, grinning.

No one spoke up.

"Yeah, as I was saying, we all know Sean loves his independence," Tom said and sipped his coffee before continuing. "It's why he operated his own gaming business. He's more comfortable left to his own devices. He'd rather work by himself. I think, though, I've been able to convince him to stay on the island and help me manage the Spring House so we can both have some freedom. Plus knowing he has Heather here now," Tom tapped her hand, "I'm kinda hoping it's another reason for him to stay."

"I'm staying," Sean said, grinning and taking Heather's hand in his own. "And yes, I will continue helping you."

"Yay!" Tom said. He glanced at Amanda saying, "Now what I need is someone to help me with my social media presence. Would you consider helping me now that you've committed your business talents to helping island folk only?"

A woman with closely cropped hair moved her chair away from her table. She stood up and announced, "I'm Cheryl Ball and this is Ed. If it wasn't for your friend Amanda, we wouldn't be sitting here today as a couple. I don't know what she did or how, but Amanda increased our realty business by at least three-fold. And she helped me understand Ed's training." She winked at Ed. "In fact, our business has been so successful that we are now looking for office space closer to downtown."

Helen Johnson, the manager of Mohegan Café, spoke up too. "I hired Amanda to help with my social media presence. Since she's been on the job, I've seen an uptick in my business as well. I didn't think after being in the same place for all these years, I could possibly see new business. But I have. I know it's due to Amanda's influence." Helen picked up her coffee cup and raised it in salutation to Amanda. "I've overheard tourists I've never seen before mention a social media post that brought them here. See," she said, "Amanda helps our little island survive in this modern world." Cheryl then nodded to Tom. "I think you'd make an excellent partnership."

Amanda felt her face flush with embarrassment. Not used to this praise, she didn't know how to react. Looking across the table at Ester, she pleaded with her eyes.

"You got this," Ester mouthed.

Drawing in a breath, Amanda turned back to everyone. "I don't know what to say. I'm only doing my job, but I appreciate all the compliments."

While sitting next to her sister, Rylee, Teagan leaned over. Whispering in Rylee's ear, she said, "Maybe we should use Amanda for our interior design business."

"Thinking the same thing, Teagan." Rylee finished her coffee and put the cup back on the table. "There are a lot of old houses that could use some fresh paint."

Smiling, Teagan said, "I like it." Alex leaned over and gave Riley a kiss. It took Teagan a moment to understand what had just transpired. When she did, her mouth fell open. "Wait a minute," she said. "What's this... have you finally figured out what everyone else has seen for years?"

"Thanks to Michelle Joy and Into the Past," Riley said glancing at Alex.

Over hearing Michelle's name, Ester chimed in. "I've known Michelle for over ten years. When she discovered my husband Hoffy had passed, Michelle wanted to put me under her spell."

"Wanted to?" Teagan asked. "Sounds like it didn't happen."

Ester closed her eyes, smiling. "It didn't. Didn't have to. We loved each other in our own way, in this life. I didn't need evidence or verification. Just like I love all of you. You've become my family. And I want to thank you for today. But not just for today." Ester drew in a breath. Attempting not to break down, she sighed and said, "Thank you for being you. And thank you for my birthday celebration. It's been one of the best things that could have happened today. I love you all."

Tom walked around the table and sat down beside Ester. "We love you too." He took Ester's hand. "You're just as important to us. Maybe more so. You've already seen how you influenced so many of us and how much Teagan's come to rely on you. You may not know this, but you were the first person on Block Island who befriended me when I arrived. You took time to show me around. And once you realized I wanted to move here and look for a business to manage, you were the first person to mention the Spring House being on the market. You've done so much more for the people sitting here than anything we could possibly do in return. Celebrating your birthday is just one small thing we can do for you." Tom looked down at his watch and said, "I think I've left the inn in capable hands, but I should get back. Happy birthday, Ester. So glad we were able to share this day with you." He moved away from the table and gave her a kiss on the cheek.

Once Tom left, Alex decided to share the big news. "Shall we tell the whole story?" he asked Rylee. Before she could respond he plunged ahead. "Michelle helped us realize we've always been together. That we choose our lives, our families, our lovers and friends before we incarnate. Rylee and I," he gazed at her and smiled, "just took longer to understand that. We've always been together, Rylee and I. In fact, we spent one life here on Block Island. It's how we discovered our intertwined lives.

Rylee interjected here. "Alex started a gravestone rubbing at Island Cemetery when he found someone who shared his birthdate. We learned later we were that couple."

"You're talking about reincarnation?" Teagan asked. "When did you find out you had been here before?"

"I don't know." Rylee played with her hair, twirling a few strands around her index finger. "I guess I always wondered. Especially since Uncle Chris seemed certain of it. I remember the books he had me read on the topic. Some were indisputable." She drew in a breath. Looking up at Alex and squeezing his hand tighter, she said, "Then there's Alex here. I didn't realize how close we were." She kissed his cheek again.

"Do you know," Alex said, "Rylee called me Anima Mia first? It must have stuck with me somewhere in my subconscious. We discovered that while Michelle had me under hypnosis. So much has happened in the past couple of days, I'm still having a difficult time understanding." He reached across the table and took Rylee's hand, holding on so tightly, afraid to let go, for fear of losing the newfound feelings they were having. He smiled then at Ester.

Ester stood up and stepped away from the table. "I'm so happy you worked this out. I should really head back home. Can I expect you tonight, Teagan?"

"Oh yeah," she said. "I'm not planning on going anywhere today. Golden Grove will be waiting. I'll probably start moving stuff over by the middle of the month and hopefully to be fully moved in by the middle of October."

With everything resolved, Bruce took the time to thank all the people there. "Without everyone here now, I certainly wouldn't be the success I've become. Much like Ester, you've all become more like family to me. I love you all. Now get outta here and enjoy the rest of the day."

Sean and Heather started to walk down the stairs to the street below when Bruce cleared his throat. "Ummm... where are you going, Heather?" he asked with a grin.

Heather turned back. "Just walking Sean to the street."

"Go ahead. Have fun," Bruce said. "Just be back by three to begin dinner prep."

Teagan, Rylee, Alex, and Amanda were still seated at the tables. "Do you want a ride home, Ester?"

"Nah. Too nice to be in a car. I want to take advantage of the weather while we have it." Ester stood up, walked closer to Teagan, and hugged her. "Thank you for today." Shaking her head, she smiled. "You are the best."

The front porch emptied as Ester walked down the stairs and Bruce went back to the kitchen. This gave Teagan an opening to broach the subject of partnering with Amanda. "So," she said. "What do you think of partnering up? Rylee and I have a good following on the mainland, but we could definitely use your expertise here."

"I like it," Amanda said. "I'll start getting word out immediately that there are two new designers in town."

With that settled, they stepped away from the table and made their way down the steps to the street below.

Smiling, Teagan thought about her future on Block Island. James and Sean seemed to have reconciled. She made several new friends and reacquainted herself with Ester. Yes, indeed. Magic surged through all of Block Island. Spiritual, ethereal, gossamer. By any name, magic lived here. From goose bumps appearing on tourists and locals alike upon touching Block Island ground to the real thing—reuniting Amanda and her grandfather earlier this summer.

Teagan felt sure there were more stories just waiting to be told, and now she had plenty of time to listen for them. Keeping her eyes and ears open felt like the key to unlocking these stories. She couldn't wait to start. Who knows? Teagan may return to an earlier passion she had when growing up.

Writing always made her happy as a young girl, and her school teachers had said she had a gift for expressing herself in writing. Block Island may bring that back. As she walked to Finn's, Teagan started formulating a plan. Smiling, she finally understood why this place became such an obsession for so many. More than the locals, more than the rocky coastline, it was the magic that permeated the entire island.

That's what drew her Uncle Chris here. And ultimately, it's what hooked Teagan, and likely Rylee, Sean, and James as well. Only a select lucky few heard that clarion call, and Teagan felt blessed to be among them.

When she arrived back at Ester's, Teagan sat on the front porch. A phrase from *Rhyme of the Ancient Mariner* flitted through her head.

"Water, water, every where."

You couldn't go far without seeing water.

Broken from her reverie by the front door opening, Teagan turned to see Ester standing at the threshold.

"Did you tell Bruce about my birthday?" she asked, smiling.

"Nope," Teagan said. "You brought that on yourself. You aren't good at lying. You told me not to tell anyone and I didn't."

"Yeah," Ester said, walking out and closing the door behind her. She sat down in the chair beside Teagan. Laughing now, she said, "Guess I did." She gazed out at the sea and couldn't help but think about how fortunate she felt to call Block Island her home. To have friends she called family? Well, that was a bonus.

Ester said, "This is heaven. Where else can you step outside your house and see the sun set on the water? End of a perfect day." She reached across and took Teagan's hand in hers. "End of a perfect season. So happy you spent it here."

They closed their eyes, each thinking about the ethereal and physical connection they felt for each other. Two rocks on a beach, connected by sand. Two islands in a sea, connected beneath still waters.

Block Island magic brought them together. Of that, they were both sure.

Magic permeated Block Island. You could find it anywhere. You only needed to know where to look.

253 C. Jennings Penders

Acknowledgements

A writer's life is solitary. That doesn't mean, however, that a writer works in a vacuum. There have been so many people who have been influential: **Tim Jacobs** and I have been friends since the late 1980s. He has helped make each of these stories stronger. His editing service, JWC Publishing, has been amazing. Everyone needs an editor — not just to find errors but to look for places where something is missing. Tim has done both for me.

Jennifer Christiansen, an editor at JWC Publishing did a line by line edit of *Arrivals and Departures*, giving the book a more polished edit.

Jason Marchi is not just a close friend. He is also my publisher, with a keen sense about what makes a story work. Like Tim, I've known Jason since the late 1980s. They were in my first writers' group.

Juliana Gribbins is another writer I've known since the early 1990s and has been a huge help in improving my writing.

The staff at the EC Scranton Memorial Library in Madison, Connecticut has also given me valuable advice: from Clara Flath who helped me find a pet name for one of my story characters in "Together." Bonny Albanese has been my friend and coworker for almost as long as I've worked at The Scranton Library. She's also been a help with this manuscript, agreeing to read through it and look for grammatical errors.

The Block Island Facebook Group has answered every question I've posed to them. Without all the help I've received, this book surely would not have come to fruition in the state that it has.

Writing is solitary, but no writer works in a vacuum. That fact can be seen from everyone who has helped me here.

I also have to mention four other writers who have been instrumental in their support: Gary Braver, Mark Brewer, Suzanne Palmieri, and Gina Heron. These four people have continued to cheer me on and have quickly become valuable friends to me. I appreciate their support as well as everyone mentioned above.

Made in United States
North Haven, CT
09 June 2023

37547609R00157